Devlin

7 Brides for 7 Blackthornes #1

BARBARA FREETHY

BARBARA
FREETHY
—BOOKS—

Fog City Publishing

PRAISE FOR BARBARA FREETHY

"A fabulous, page-turning combination of romance and intrigue. Fans of Nora Roberts and Elizabeth Lowell will love this book." — *NYT Bestselling Author Kristin Hannah on Golden Lies*

"Freethy is at the top of her form. Fans of Nora Roberts will find a similar tone here, framed in Freethy's own spare, elegant style." — *Contra Costa Times on Summer Secrets*

"Freethy hits the ground running as she kicks off another winning romantic suspense series…Freethy is at her prime with a superb combo of engaging characters and gripping plot." — *Publishers' Weekly on Silent Run*

"I love the Callaways! Heartwarming romance, intriguing suspense and sexy alpha heroes. What more could you want?" — *NYT Bestselling Author Bella Andre*

"I adore the Callaways, a family we'd all love to have. Each new book is a deft combination of emotion, suspense and family dynamics." — *Bestselling Author Barbara O'Neal*

"Once I start reading a Callaway novel, I can't put it down. Fast-paced action, a poignant love story and a tantalizing mystery in every book!" — *USA Today Bestselling Author Christie Ridgway*

PRAISE FOR BARBARA FREETHY

"Barbara Freethy is a master storyteller with a gift for spinning tales about ordinary people in extraordinary situations." — *Romance Reviews Today*

"PERILOUS TRUST is a non-stop thriller that seamlessly melds jaw-dropping suspense with sizzling romance. I was riveted from the first page to the last." — *USA Today*

"Freethy (Silent Fall) has a gift for creating complex, appealing characters and emotionally involving, often suspenseful stories." — *Library Journal on Suddenly One Summer*

Freethy hits the ground running as she kicks off another winning romantic suspense series...Freethy is at her prime with a superb combo of engaging characters and gripping plot." — P*ublishers' Weekly on Silent Run*

"If you love nail-biting suspense and heartbreaking emotion, Silent Run belongs on the top of your to-be-bought list. I could not turn the pages fast enough." — *NYT Bestselling Author Mariah Stewart*

"Hooked me from the start and kept me turning pages throughout all the twists and turns." — *NYT Bestselling Author JoAnn Ross*

ALSO BY BARBARA FREETHY

7 BRIDES FOR 7 BLACKTHORNES

Devlin – Barbara Freethy (#1)

Jason – Julia London (#2)

Ross – Lynn Raye Harris (#3)

Phillip – Cristin Harber (#4)

Brock – Roxanne St. Claire (#5)

Logan – Samantha Chase (#6)

Trey – Christie Ridgway (#7)

Don't Miss My New Contemporary Series:
WHISPER LAKE

Always With Me (#1)

My Wildest Dream (#2)

For a complete list of books, visit www.barbarafreethy.com

DEVLIN

CHAPTER ONE

"YOU ARE ONE COLD, ruthless, heartless, horrible person," Hannah Reid declared, her practiced speech going out of her head as soon as Devlin Blackthorne made the mistake of giving her a charming smile and saying hello as if nothing had happened.

"Nice to see you, too, Hannah," Devlin said, his brown-eyed gaze filling with wariness. "How long has it been? Three, four years?"

"Five."

"No wonder you look so much older. I think you had just graduated from college last time I saw you. How come you haven't come back before this?"

"That is not important. Don't try to distract me. I want to know what's going on. Why did you fire my father?"

"It wasn't my decision; my dad terminated Frank."

"Terminated?" she echoed. "My father has worked for Blackthorne Boatworks for thirty years. It's his boat designs that have made this company famous. He is its heart and its soul." She'd never felt so much anger. Ever since she'd heard about her father's abrupt firing, her fury had grown to an explosive level. It had pushed her to get on a plane and fly from Texas to Maine, and the travel time had done nothing to lessen her anger.

"I agree. Frank has been the heart and soul of this company," Devlin said, appearing to choose his words carefully.

"Yes, he has. Which is why this makes no sense. He devoted his life to your family business. He ruined his marriage, he shattered my family, all because of his dedication to the job he loved and to your family. And you just let him go? You throw him away like an old newspaper? How could you do that?"

"You're not listening, Hannah. It was my father's doing."

"Your father doesn't run the company; you do."

"My father runs every company within Blackthorne Enterprises," he snapped, his brown eyes darkening. "He has the ultimate say."

"So, talk to him. Tell him he's wrong."

"Tell him he's wrong? No one tells Graham Blackthorne he's wrong, least of all one of his sons."

"Then I'll tell him. Where is he?"

Devlin smiled. "I think you would actually do that."

"You're damned right I would. I'm not afraid of your father."

"Look, Hannah, I've already told my father to hire Frank back. He says it's between Frank and him. He also told me that Frank knows what he has to do if he wants his job back."

"What the hell does that mean? He works endless hours. What more could he possibly do for you?"

"Honestly, I think whatever is between them is personal, because neither one will tell me what their argument was about. I've asked both of them several times." He paused. "Have you asked Frank? Did he give you a reason?"

She frowned, wishing she could give Devlin a different answer. "He said that your family didn't value him, respect him, or trust his word. He wasn't just angry; he was hurt.

Actually, he was devastated. I've never heard him sound so bleak. It scared me. I jumped on a plane as soon as I could."

Devlin's brows knit together in puzzlement. "I don't know what he's talking about. I've expressed my gratitude and respect for his work many times. He has to be referring to my father."

"Regardless, my dad needs his job back."

"That will happen with a little time."

"How much time? My father isn't rich. He's not a Blackthorne. You have to talk to your father again, make him see reason."

"Does Frank know you're here?" he asked curiously.

"He knows I'm in King Harbor. I got in last night."

"But he doesn't know you're here at the office talking to me."

"I might not have mentioned it," she admitted.

A knowing gleam entered his eyes. "Because he wouldn't want you to fight his battles for him."

"He's not fighting; that's the problem. He drank half the night at the Vault, and I don't think he slept at all. He's like a shadow of himself. I'm worried."

"I'm sorry to hear that. I really am."

"Then do something," she said, waving her hand in frustration. She couldn't stand that Devlin was so calm. Actually, she couldn't stand that he was so attractive.

How was it possible that he'd gotten more attractive with age? He was thirty-one now; he should be graying or balding or putting on weight, but his light-brown hair was thick and wavy, his brown eyes flecked with sparkling gold, his body looking fit and toned in his T-shirt and faded jeans.

All the Blackthorne brothers and cousins were good-looking guys, but Devlin's grinning, charismatic smile, his wind-blown brown hair, often sunburned face, and his love of the sea had always made him incredibly attractive to her.

Not that he'd ever looked in her direction. He was five

years older than her, and after her parents had divorced when she was twelve, she'd only been in King Harbor for a few weeks every summer. Back then when she'd seen Devlin, he'd usually had some cute girl or two by his side.

Her gut tightened, and she wanted to stop looking at him, but she couldn't seem to pull her gaze away—not until a flicker of amusement entered his eyes.

Then she forced herself to clear her throat and glance toward the window. She could see a boat on the lift, ready to be lowered into the water. "Is that the *Wind Warrior*—this year's entry in the Southern Maine Sailing Invitational?"

"Yes. She's ready for a test run."

"A run my father should be making. Do you really think you can win the race without him? He's been on every winning boat you've ever sailed. Even though your family keeps the trophy, it's as much his as it is yours."

Devlin stared back at her. "You've got a massive chip on your shoulder, Hannah."

"Your family put it there." She wasn't just talking about her father's recent termination. Her resentment of the Blackthornes ran deep. Even though it probably wasn't fair, she blamed them for the break-up of her family. If they hadn't put such tremendous demands on her father, he wouldn't have had to work all the time.

"I am sorry about what happened," Devlin said.

"Then talk to your dad. Get him to change his mind."

"I will do that."

"When?"

"I'm seeing him tonight for my mom's sixtieth birthday party. But I have to tell you that our fathers are as obstinate as they come. Neither one ever wants to back down. What you or I want probably isn't going to factor into this situation."

She couldn't say he was wrong about that. "My dad can be bullheaded, but it's that stubbornness that also drives his perfection at work."

A loud crash reverberated through the building, and Devlin winced. "I need to get back to work." As he came around the desk, he added, "Frank said you're in real estate now."

"Yes. I work as an agent in my mother's firm."

"I remember how much you loved being on the water. When you came to visit your father in the summers, you always wanted to be out on a boat."

"Yes, I did." She was surprised he remembered that, and as their gazes clung together, an odd tingle ran down her spine.

She'd come into his office full of fire, but the sparks were changing from anger into something else…something she should not be feeling. Devlin was her father's boss; she could not forget that.

Clearing her throat, she said, "You will speak to your father?"

"I said I would. How long are you staying in town?"

"I'm not sure. It depends on what happens with my dad."

"Why don't I walk you out?"

"I can find my way," she said, as they moved toward the door. "Although, it seems busier here than I remember."

"We've been expanding the last several years," he said, waving her through the doorway.

Devlin's office was on the second floor of the massive building, which was about twenty-thousand square feet. Two additional offices, one belonging to her father, another to the operations manager, as well as a conference room, lined the interior hallway overlooking the first-floor workspace.

Downstairs, the cavernous room allowed for construction and restoration of yachts, with separate spaces for carpentry, painting, rigging, and mechanical services. Enormous doors opened onto a ramp with a lift and a deep-water dock behind the building. Blackthorne Boatworks was a full-service operation offering everything from design to new construction, restoration, service, and sales.

As they walked down the stairs, she saw two boats currently in progress: one a skeletal hull, the other about fifty percent done. There were at least six men working between the two projects.

Her father should be there, too. He was a master craftsman. He wasn't only a designer; he was also a builder, and a sailor.

"You can't afford to lose my dad," she told Devlin as they reached the bottom of the stairs. "He's brilliant."

"It wouldn't be easy, but no one is irreplaceable."

Her anger returned. "Now you sound like your father's son. The Blackthornes rule the world."

Irritation ran through his eyes. "My family doesn't rule the world, but we did build our businesses from the ground up, and we worked hard to get where we are. We offer our employees excellent benefits, and Frank has been treated like a member of the family for as long as you and I have been alive." Devlin paused. "You should talk to your dad. You might be surprised that you don't know as much as you think you do about the way things are around here."

She walked slowly out to her car, hoping he wasn't right.

As Devlin left his apartment on the third floor of the Boatworks and drove to his parents' home a little before six, his mind drifted back to his earlier confrontation with Hannah Reid.

She'd certainly been hot under the collar—not that she'd been wearing a collar. No, her short, sleeveless light-blue linen dress had clung to her beautiful curves and showed off her tanned, slender legs. Her blonde hair had caught the light every time she'd shaken her head at him, and her blue eyes had shot off more than a few sparks.

He didn't remember her being so pretty. Not that he'd paid much attention to her. She was five years younger than him, which had felt like a million years when he was a teenager. Now, not so much…

But his unexpected attraction was a non-starter. He wasn't going to mess around with Hannah. He had enough problems. Not that she'd mess around with him. She clearly didn't think highly of anyone with Blackthorne for their last name.

While he respected her for standing up for her dad, it was clear she didn't have any idea of the dynamics between Frank and his father. Those two had always butted heads, but at times they'd also been friends.

Apparently, now they were enemies, and he had no idea why.

His father refused to discuss it with him. But he would have to bring it up again, not just because he'd promised Hannah, but also because he needed Frank back at work.

They had orders to fill and designs to be finished, and, as Hannah had pointed out, Frank had always helped him race their newest boat in the Southern Maine Sailing Invitational, which brought together racers from all over the world on Memorial Day weekend.

He'd never sailed the race without Frank, and while he knew he could do it, he would miss him. It wouldn't be the same.

Although…this would be a good time to get his father on board. But while his father had a shelf of trophies from the race, they were all from more than a decade ago. His father had quit racing after his brother Mark and his wife had passed away in a tragic plane crash, leaving behind three boys, who had subsequently been raised by his parents.

His father had always sailed the race with Mark, and he'd

never wanted to do it with anyone else—not even his own son. But then, he and his father didn't do much of anything together, whether it was on a boat or not. It wasn't that they were estranged or anything; they just didn't have much in common.

Usually, his dad left the management of the Boatworks to him, which made this Frank situation even more bothersome. Frank had to have done something fairly big for his dad to have stepped in the way he had. But hopefully, he'd had enough time to cool off and be open to reason.

He turned in to the driveway of the Blackthorne Estate and parked off to the side, preferring to have his car more readily available when he wanted to leave. Soon there would be a crush of vehicles in front of the house.

Getting out of the car, he walked down the drive, appreciating the unusually warm evening, and he also found himself looking forward to the night ahead. It was his mother's sixtieth birthday, and the entire family would be there, including his three brothers, three cousins, and his grandmother. They hadn't all been together since Christmas, and it would be nice to see the house full of Blackthornes again.

As the three-story mansion came into view, he smiled to himself, thinking that the word *house* had always been an understatement. The fifteen-thousand-square-foot home had been built by his grandparents, funded by Blackthorne Gold, the whisky that had built the Blackthorne empire. Surrounded by lush gardens, the mansion also boasted a white widow's walk overlooking the sea.

Growing up, the house had always been their summer base. During the year, they'd lived in an equally impressive home in Boston. And Boston was where many of his family members still resided. He, however, had decided to take over the Boatworks five years ago, making his life and business interests much more suited to King Harbor and the Maine coast. While he could have lived at the estate, he'd felt a need for his own space, and the apartment over the Boatworks was more convenient and more his style.

When he reached the front door, he ran into Trey, his oldest brother. "You made it. When did you get in?" He gave Trey a hug, then grinned at his brother's always stiff response.

They were only three years apart in age, but they were light-years apart in everything else. Trey was executive vice president of operations for Blackthorne Enterprises, and he was all business, all the time. Even for tonight's party, he looked every inch the executive in his expensive designer suit. His face was cleanly shaven, and his brown hair was neatly trimmed and styled so that not a hair was out of place. Looking at Trey now, he could hardly believe this was the same kid who had once built forts with him out of blankets and chairs.

"I got in an hour ago." Trey straightened his tie and gave him a frown. "You couldn't dress up for this, Devlin?"

"You're not in Boston anymore, Trey. This is King Harbor." He thought his tan slacks and light-blue button-down shirt were perfect for his mom's sixtieth birthday party. "And it's just family and a few close friends."

"Actually, that's not true. Not just the family is coming."

"What are you talking about?"

"Dad invited some of our business associates to the party."

"Like who?"

"The McKinney brothers."

He raised an eyebrow. The McKinney brothers distributed rival whisky brands around the country. "Dad hates the McKinney brothers."

"Not since we made them an offer to acquire their company. It would be a coup to take over their distribution network."

"I can't believe they want to sell."

"The older McKinney is battling cancer, and his younger brother wants to retire to Hawaii. They think it might be time to get out. None of their sons or daughters are interested in taking over the company." Trey paused, giving him a sharp look. "I'm surprised you didn't know that. We've been talking about it for months."

"I've been busy lately."

"We're all busy. You should pay more attention to the whisky business. It's what funds the Boatworks."

He didn't rise to Trey's bait. He didn't care that his business wasn't the biggest moneymaker in the company; he was doing what he loved, and that was enough. He'd learned early on that life was short—sometimes brutally short.

"Let's go inside," he said, opening the door for his brother.

As they stepped into the entry, he could hear laughter and conversation coming from the living room. Before they could move in that direction, his cousin Brock came jogging down the stairs.

Like Trey, Brock was also in a suit, as befitting the senior vice president of brand management and the keeper of the Blackthorne brand.

"Devlin," Brock said with a welcoming smile. "Good to see you."

"You, too. Trey was telling me this isn't just a birthday party but also a business meeting."

"Your father likes to multitask," Brock replied with a shrug. "But we'll make sure it doesn't take away from Aunt Claire's birthday."

"I hope so," he murmured.

"I want to talk to you, Brock, before we see Dad," Trey said. "Devlin, do you mind?"

"Go ahead. The last thing I want to do is talk business right now."

As his brother and cousin walked down the hall, the front door opened and two more Blackthornes entered the house: his cousins, Jason and Phillip. Jason wore jeans and a white T-shirt under a navy-blue blazer and had his phone pressed to his ear. He gave him a vague wave as he walked by.

"Devlin," Phillip said with a smile, giving him a hearty hug. "Good to see you."

"You, too. Did you come with Jason?"

"No. We met in the driveway, but he's been on the phone since he got out of the car, so I haven't actually spoken to him. He's in the midst of some TV negotiation. How's Aunt Claire? Is she feeling sixty?"

"I think this birthday might be bothering her a little."

"Really?" Phillip said with surprise. "She looks great."

"I know, but she mentioned to me the other day that sixty feels old to her. She seemed a little down."

"Well, hopefully this party will cheer her up. I have to admit I'm not used to seeing Aunt Claire in any kind of a down mood. She always has a smile on her face and is ready to deal with whatever life sends her way—like three orphaned teenage boys. I'll never be able to express my gratitude for the way she took in Jason, Brock and myself when our parents died."

"She didn't hesitate for even a second. Nor did my father." Graham wasn't always the most generous man, but when it came to family, he was incredibly loyal.

"Let's find the party. I could use a drink."

He followed Jason into the immense living room, which boasted a massive stone fireplace, two separate seating areas, and floor-to-ceiling windows offering impressive ocean views. There were about a dozen people in the room as well as two servers offering appetizers and glasses of champagne.

"Looks like the bar is on the patio," Phillip said, waving his hand toward the open French doors. "You want a beer or a whisky? Or are you going to have champagne?"

"A beer would be great."

As Phillip moved onto the patio, Devlin saw his youngest brother Logan talking to a very attractive redhead. Logan gave him a grinning nod and went back to his conversation. At least one of his brothers was here to have a good time.

A moment later, Phillip handed him an ice-cold bottle of beer.

"What is with Brock and Trey?" Phillip asked. "They look like they're going to a business meeting."

"Apparently, they are. My father invited some associates to the party." He frowned as his dad left his mother to join Brock, Trey and the McKinney brothers by the fireplace. "Mom doesn't look happy about it."

"I can't see why she would be," Phillip murmured. "Your father doesn't know when to shut it down."

"No, he does not. Let's talk to her."

They walked across the room, and his mother broke away from her conversation to give them both hugs and kisses.

"Happy birthday, Mom," he said.

"Thank you, honey." She turned to her nephew. "Phillip, I'm so glad you could come."

"I wouldn't miss it, Aunt Claire. You look beautiful. Not a day over thirty."

"You've always been a good liar," she said with a laugh.

"True. But tonight I only tell the truth," Phillip joked.

His mom let out a small sigh as her gaze moved to her husband. "I wish that was true of all the Blackthornes."

"Is something wrong, Mom?" he asked.

"Yes." She turned back to him. "I did not invite the McKinney brothers to my party. I can't believe your father is turning my birthday into another business opportunity. Actually, I can believe it; I'm just incredibly disappointed. I told him it was important to me to have all my friends and family together. But not only is he doing business, he has pulled Brock and Trey into it as well."

"We'll still have a good time," he said, trying to distract her.

"Yes," she murmured, but her gaze had lost its sparkle.

"Jason is here, too," Phillip put in.

"I saw him walk out to the patio, but I haven't had a chance to say hello; he's been on the phone the whole time. More business. Everyone has something else they'd rather be doing," she complained.

"I'll get my brother off the phone," Phillip offered.

"Oh, it doesn't matter," she said, waving her hand in defeat. "I've finally given up."

His gaze narrowed at her words. "What does that mean, Mom?"

"You two—you and Phillip—you've always done what you wanted to do, followed your dreams. Phillip stepped away from the business despite the family pressure. And you, Devlin, you work your passion—the boats, the sailing. It's not just a job to you; it's your dream."

"You encouraged me to follow my dreams."

"I did. Perhaps I should have taken my own advice. It's important to do what you love, or at least to find out what you love. The years go very quickly, faster than you'll know until you get to be my age. Then you realize everything is behind you."

"There's a lot in front of you, too," he reminded her. "Are you all right, Mom? Is there something I can do? You seem a little upset."

"I thought this party would be different. Do you remember your father's sixtieth birthday party? Or the one he had last year for sixty-five?"

"I remember them both. We celebrated sixty in Monaco on a yacht and sixty-five in London with a few royals in the crowd." He paused. "Did you want a bigger party?"

"It's not about the party; it's about the intent."

He didn't know what she was talking about, but she was

definitely worked up about something, and he had a feeling his dad was in the doghouse. "Tonight will be fun. We're all together."

"Are we?" she asked cryptically. A glint of determination entered her eyes. "You know, Devlin, I think I've finally realized that the only person who can make me feel better is me. Will you excuse me?"

"Of course, but where are you going?"

"To do something I should have done a long time ago."

He wanted to ask her what that could possibly be, but she was already on her way out of the living room.

"What was that about?" Phillip asked with concern. "She seems very angry with Uncle Graham."

"She does." His parents had been married for thirty-seven years and while they'd had their share of arguments, they'd always seemed very solid. "Maybe it's just her birthday. She's feeling her age."

"Well, you might want to give your father a heads-up."

"I will, as soon as he gets done talking to the McKinney brothers. He won't hear me if he's trying to make a deal." He paused as his youngest brother Logan joined them.

"What's going on with Mom?" Logan asked. "She flew out of the room like a woman on a mission."

"I'm not sure. She seems to be upset with Dad for turning this party into a business meeting."

"What else is new?" Logan drawled. "It's Dad. It's what he does. She knows that."

"Maybe I should go talk to her," he said, not really sure he wanted to deal with his mother in the mood she was in. Before he could move, his grandmother, Fiona Blackthorne joined them.

The white-haired Fiona was dressed in a bright floral dress, her face perfectly made up, and long dangly earrings adding a bit of fun. At eighty-six, Fiona enjoyed being herself in as many bright colors as possible.

"Nana," he said, giving her a kiss. "You look very pretty."

"I know I do," she said with a happy smile. "Thanks for noticing, Devlin. Where is your mother?"

"I'm not sure. She walked out of the room a few minutes ago. She's unhappy that Dad is doing business tonight."

Fiona's gaze moved to Graham, and she sighed. "My son can be an idiot."

"I can't disagree."

"Sometimes I wonder how he has managed to hang on to Claire for as long as he has. She has always been a beautiful and popular lady. He had to work hard to get her attention in the first place. She had all kind of suitors back in the day. But he was determined to win her, and he did. I'm not sure he's putting in that same kind of effort now." She paused, her gaze moving back to them. "Anyway, what is going on with all of you? Any new ladies? Logan, I saw you talking to a very pretty woman," Fiona said with a sly smile in Logan's direction. "Did you bring her with you?"

Logan grinned. "No. That's actually Rhea Holmes, Tom and Laura's daughter."

"Oh, goodness, I didn't even recognize her. So, she's not your date."

"No, I came on my own." Fiona turned to Phillip. "And you, dear?"

"No news. Just working away."

"You're still enjoying the non-profit sector?"

"Absolutely. Sending kids who have suffered a tragic loss to camp is the best thing I've ever done."

"Who better to understand the loss of a parent than you," Fiona said gently. "Mark and Julie would be so proud of you, Phillip."

"I hope so."

His grandmother's gaze came to rest on him. "I hear you've been burning the midnight oil at the Boatworks."

"I have. Not only is the race coming up in two weeks, but

we also have quite a few orders that need to be finished before summer is officially here, and now I'm shorthanded."

"Yes, what happened with Frank Reid?" she asked with a gleam of curiosity. "I don't understand why he's no longer working there."

"You'd have to ask Dad. He fired Frank, and he won't tell me why. But he needs to rehire him as soon as possible."

"Wait," Logan cut in, surprise in his eyes. "Dad fired Frank? That's crazy. He's been with the business for thirty years. He is the business—no offense, Devlin."

"None taken. I agree. No one matches Frank in experience and loyalty to the company."

"Well, your father seems to be causing a lot of turmoil these days," Fiona said, with an unhappy shake of her head. "I don't think it's deliberate. But he gets busy and wrapped up in his own ideas, and he takes people for granted. One of you should go get Claire. She needs to be here, surrounded by her friends and family."

"I could do that," he said.

"You don't have to," Logan interrupted. "Mom is back, but something is wrong."

His gaze moved to the doorway where his mother stood. She was no longer wearing her party dress but rather dark jeans and a sweater. And as she stepped over the threshold, he thought he saw a suitcase on the floor behind her. His gut tightened.

She clapped her hands, drawing everyone's attention.

"Thank you all for coming to my party," she said loudly. "I hope you enjoy yourselves. There's plenty of food and drinks. And I know some of you haven't seen each other in a while, so this will be a good time for you to catch up. But as for me, I'll be leaving."

"What?" Graham asked, his booming voice ringing out across the room.

His mother's gaze swung to Graham. She put up a hand as he started forward.

"No," she said, shaking her head. "Not this time. You won't talk me out of it. I'm leaving, Graham. Inviting your business associates to my birthday party was the last straw. I have given you my life for the last thirty-seven years—"

"Claire—"

"It's my turn to talk."

"Then let's go in the other room."

"Why? Because this party doesn't just include the family and close friends that I requested?"

"You're making a scene," Graham barked.

"Well, it's my party; I get to do that, don't I?"

"What is going on?" he hissed.

"I'll tell you," she said, her voice choking with emotion as she looked at her husband. "I have done everything you wanted, Graham. I have supported you in every possible way. I have been there since day one. I have seen you through every hardship, every business deal, every joy, every pain. And I always thought that one day you would be there for me, that it would be my turn, but even after I told you how worrying this birthday was for me, you decided that business was more important. Well, I'm done putting my life on hold. I've been by your side, in your shadow for way too long. I've kept your secret, even when I knew I shouldn't. It's too much. I can't do it anymore."

"Claire, stop," Graham commanded.

"I will stop talking, because it's time for me to leave. It's time for me to put myself first. Don't try to stop me, Graham."

She turned and walked out of the room, leaving shocked silence behind her. His father seemed frozen for a moment, but then he stomped out of the room.

Devlin moved toward the doorway, crossing the threshold

just in time to see his mother walk out the front door, accompanied by their handyman, Joe O'Reilly, who was carrying her suitcase.

"Do not drive her anywhere, Joe," Graham ordered.

Joe shrugged. "Sorry. She asked."

"Don't take this out on him," Claire told Graham. "Go back to your party."

"It's your party," Graham said. "This is ridiculous, Claire. You're acting crazy."

Devlin winced at his father's thoughtless words.

His mother slammed the door in his father's face.

Graham's hands clenched into fists, and for a minute Devlin thought his dad would go after her, but then he turned around and saw everyone looking at him. In typical Blackthorne style, he threw back his shoulders, lifted his chin and faced the crowd head-on.

"It will be fine," his father said loudly, confidently. "Claire is having a bit of trouble coming to terms with her birthday, entering a new decade and all that. Don't worry. She'll be back. Please, drink, eat, enjoy being with each other, as Claire asked you to do."

He had to admit he was impressed with his father's ability to spin the situation so quickly.

The front door opened, and his father started, clearly thinking Claire had changed her mind and come back.

But it wasn't his mother who stepped into the entry; it was his younger brother Ross, who was late, as usual.

"Hello," Ross began cheerfully, then stopped, obviously taking in the tension in the room. "What did I miss?"

His father just shook his head. "I'm sure someone will fill you in, Ross." Then he brushed by Devlin, taking the crowd back into the living room.

"Seriously, what did I miss?" Ross asked him.

"Not much," he replied dryly. "Except Mom just left Dad."

"What? You're kidding, right?"

"You should try to be on time once in a while."

"Mom is really gone? Where?"

His gaze moved toward the front door. "I have no idea."

CHAPTER TWO

DESPITE HIS FATHER'S encouragement for their guests to enjoy the party, within an hour, everyone was gone, including his dad. Now he was sitting around the large table on the patio, with his three brothers, three cousins, and his grandmother, who was pouring them each a glass of Blackthorne Gold whisky.

"It's all going to be fine," Fiona told them. "Graham and Claire will work things out."

He wanted to believe that, but he wasn't so sure, and he saw doubt on a few other faces, along with some guilt.

"I had no idea Mom would be that upset about the McKinney brothers coming to the party," Trey said.

"Nor did I," Brock put in. "It's not like we haven't done business at parties before."

"I didn't even get a chance to speak to Claire," Jason said, more guilt in his eyes. "I was on the phone when she tried to speak to me."

"None of you are to blame for what happened tonight," Fiona said, drawing their attention back to her. "Obviously, your father has been taking your mother for granted, and she had enough."

"Where do you think she went?" Logan asked curiously.

"I have no idea, but I'm sure she's fine, and she'll be back once she calms down," Fiona replied.

"I'm not so sure," he put in. "When Mom was talking to Phillip and me, she seemed quite upset with Dad, and very interested in making a change in her life. She said something to us about it being time to make herself happy. That it was her turn."

"Well, it is her turn," Fiona agreed. "That's what she just told us all."

"Along with a few other things," Brock said with a frown. "What was that secret she was talking about?"

"A secret?" Ross interjected, a questioning gleam in his eyes. "No one told me about a secret."

"Mom said something about keeping Dad's secret before she stormed out," he told Ross. "But I have no idea what it is. Does anyone else?"

There were blank looks around the table. His gaze came to rest on his grandmother. "Nana? Do you know what secret Mom has been keeping for Dad?"

"Does it have something to do with the whisky?" Brock asked.

"Oh, boys, you need to let your parents work this out between the two of them," Fiona answered. "Speculating about secrets won't make anything better."

"Which isn't an answer," he told her.

She gave him a smile. "Wasn't it?"

"If something is going to blow up the business, we need to know," Trey put in.

"Maybe you should stop being so concerned about the business," he told his brother. "And worry more about Mom and Dad."

"I am worried about them," Trey snapped back. "That's why I'm trying to figure out what's going on."

"Rumors will be flying," Brock added. "There will be a

lot of talk. I'd like to get out in front of it."

He loved Trey and Brock but sometimes they could have as much tunnel vision as his father.

"It seems to me if either of you want to know, then you should ask Dad," Logan said. "Leave Nana out of it."

"That's an excellent idea, Logan," Fiona said. "But I wouldn't ask Graham anything tonight. Give him time to cool down. Your father may sometimes be a thoughtless, stubborn mule, but I have never had any doubt about his love for your mother or her love for him. This is just a bump in the road. And no one does bumps in the road better than a Blackthorne. When times are tough, we get tougher. We came together as a family after Mark and Julie died, and we'll continue to do so, no matter what challenges are in front of us." Her gaze swept the table. "I can't tell you how proud I am of all of you. You've grown from wild boys into strong, intelligent, capable, and proud men. Let's toast to that." She raised her glass. "To the Blackthornes—to the next generation—may you be better than all who came before you."

He clinked glasses with Phillip and Trey, who were on either side of him, and then reached across the table to touch his glass to his grandmother's. She gave him a small smile. Out of this generation, he was probably the closest to Fiona, simply because he lived in Maine all year round and lately she'd been spending less and less time in Boston and more time in her cottage and her garden at the estate.

Perhaps he could get a little more out of her when they were alone. While he wasn't worried about this alleged secret hurting his business, he was worried about how it might affect the future of his family.

"Now, let's eat," Fiona added. "There's a buffet table full of food, and if I know anything about you boys, it's that you can all eat."

"Dad, you're not eating," Hannah told her father, as she watched him swirl his spoon in a big bowl of clam chowder without taking a bite. He had, however, had several long draughts of Blackthorne Gold while they'd been waiting for their meal.

She hadn't wanted to come to the Vault for dinner. The pub and the adjacent distillery were Blackthorne properties, and she would have thought the last place her father would want to dine would be any place owned by a Blackthorne. But the Vault had always been his favorite spot, and he'd told her he wasn't going to let the Blackthornes take anything else away from him.

With its paneled wood walls, parquet floors, colorful rugs, and an extensive display of liquor, the Vault was sophisticated but also warm and comfortable, and it was popular with the locals and the tourists. It also had the best chowder in town, and with the stiff ocean breezes that had kicked up after five, it was a good night for a steaming bowl of chowder.

Not that her father seemed to have any appetite at all. He looked haggard and drawn, his thinning brown hair showing more strands of gray, his blue eyes filled with shadows, his shoulders seemingly sagging under the weight of his worries. He'd always been lean, the result of long hours of physical labor and his appalling lack of focus on getting three square meals down. When he worked, he forgot to eat. She couldn't remember the last time she'd forgotten to eat. She and her father were definitely not alike in that way.

Actually, they weren't all that alike in any way. But they did share a love of boats and sailing. It was the glue that had held them together after the divorce. It was the one thing they could talk about that didn't make either one of them unhappy.

But now the boats were making her father quite depressed, and she wanted to make the problem go away; she just didn't think she could do it alone.

"Dad," she said again.

He looked up, his gaze distracted. "What?"

"I've been talking to you for five minutes. You're not eating."

"I'm not hungry," he said, setting down his spoon.

"You should try to eat." She frowned when he motioned to the waiter to refill his whisky glass. "And maybe not drink so much."

"I don't need you telling me how much I can drink, Hannah."

"I'm just worried about you. I haven't seen you like this in a very long time—not since…" Her voice drifted away as she realized bringing up the painful subject of divorce was not the best idea.

"Since what?" he challenged. "Never lost a job before, so this is a first."

"I was talking about when Mom and I left—the divorce."

"Oh, right." He let out a sigh. "I'm sorry, Hannah. You came all this way to be here for me, and I've been a grumpy bear."

"It's okay. I know you're having a difficult time." She paused, thinking back to her earlier conversation with Devlin. "Did something happen between you and Graham that precipitated him firing you?"

"Why would you ask that?" His gaze narrowed. "You didn't talk to Graham, did you?"

"No." She hesitated, and her dad's mouth tightened.

"What did you do?" he asked.

"I spoke to Devlin. I told him you're the heart and soul of his company and he'd be a fool to lose you. And I'm not sorry I said it," she added defiantly. "Because it's true."

"This is not your fight, Hannah."

"That's the thing—I don't understand why you're not fighting."

"Wouldn't do any good."

"Why not? What happened? Please talk to me. Maybe I can help."

"You can't help. You should go home, Hannah. I appreciate your support, but this isn't a situation you can fix."

"Okay, but you must have some thoughts. What are you going to do? Where are you going to work? Will you stay here in Maine?"

"Whoa, slow down." He put up his hand. "I'm still considering my options."

"I'm sure a lot of people would love to hire you. Devlin is going to feel the pain of your loss in so many ways, including the race coming up. He's never won it without you. In fact, the Blackthornes have never won it when you weren't on the boat."

"Devlin is a good sailor, a good racer."

"Not better than you."

"No. But he'll still have the best boat in the race, one I built with my own hands. The odds will be in his favor, no matter who he gets to crew with him."

"It's not right," she said, as another wave of anger washed over her. "It's your boat."

"It's a Blackthorne boat. It was their money that built it."

"But it was your design, your craftsmanship."

"You need to take a breath, Hannah."

She probably did need to slow down, but she couldn't, not with a new idea taking hold in her head. "We could enter the race and beat the Blackthornes. Take the trophy for ourselves."

He gave her a bemused look. "We? When was the last time you raced a sailboat?"

"Not for a few years, but I'm good. You taught me well. And I have two weeks to practice."

"Don't you have to get back to work?"

"I work for Mom."

"Yes, but I'm sure that doesn't mean Marianne takes it

easy on you."

"She doesn't," she admitted.

Her mother had worked hard to build a real estate business after the divorce. She'd wanted to be able to provide a good life for both of them, and she had. After college, she'd gone to work for her mom, which had been mostly good. However, her mother was driven to succeed, and she expected that same drive from Hannah. She didn't always live up to those expectations, but she'd had a good spring and had closed a sale the day before she'd come to King Harbor.

"I can take a few weeks off, Dad. I would love to race with you. And I know we'd be good together."

"You're very persuasive, but there's one rather large problem—we don't have a boat."

"Let's find one."

"It won't be easy. Every boat in King Harbor that would qualify already has a crew."

"But you know everyone in the sailing world. We can look elsewhere in Maine, maybe Portland or Kennebunkport. The entries aren't closed yet, are they?"

"Not for three more days. I could put out some feelers…"

"Let's do it. Let's beat the Blackthornes."

"I forgot what a bulldozer you can be when you get an idea in your head," he said, with humor in his eyes. "You're a little like your mother in that way."

"I think she'd say I'm like you. Or maybe all three of us are very stubborn people."

"Too stubborn for our own good probably. How is your mother?"

"She's happy. She and Tim bought a new house. They're moving in next month. It's beautiful; it has a pool and a private tennis court, and it's also close to their country club."

"It sounds nice. What about you? Do you enjoy selling houses?"

"I've found that I'm rather good at it."

"That's not what I asked."

"It's a good job."

"Hannah…"

"I like parts of it," she conceded. "Meeting people and putting them in their dream homes gives me a lot of pleasure. I do wish I had more autonomy from Mom. It's still her baby, and she doesn't give me a lot of respect."

"You should talk to her about it."

"I have. She admits she has trouble giving up control. But I don't even know if it's the job that's not making me happy; I just know that there's something missing in my life."

"You never told me what happened to Gary."

She sighed. "He went back to his ex. That's really all there is to say."

"I'm sorry."

"Me, too. Anyway, let's get back to the race. It would be fun for us to do it together and to stick it to the Blackthornes. It's a win-win."

"Only if we win. Let me think about it."

She bit back a groan of frustration. Her dad had always been a thinker, and patience was not her strength. But if she was going to get him on board, she needed to let him decide on his own.

"Hold on! Is this little Hannah?" a booming voice asked.

She turned her head to see a tall, brown-haired man moving toward their table. His weathered, ruddy skin and bright-green eyes made her jump to her feet in delight. "Uncle Joe."

Joe Crawford embraced her with a big bear hug. In his early sixties, Joe was not really her uncle, but he was one of her father's best friends, and for as long as she could remember he'd been Uncle Joe.

Joe's love of sailing had brought him and her father together years ago. Joe was an accountant by day, but on the weekends, he could always be found on one of his boats, and he was currently serving as president of the King Harbor Yacht Club, the organizer of the upcoming race. Maybe she could get him on her side.

"I can't believe you're back in King Harbor," Joe said, as he released her. "You stayed away a long time."

"After college, my summers were no longer free. Can you join us?"

"I can." He pulled a chair over to their table and sat down. "When did you get in, Hannah?"

"Yesterday."

"That's great. How long are you staying?"

"I'm not sure, but probably through Memorial Day."

"You'll be here for the race?"

"I will. Dad and I were just talking about it. We're thinking of racing together. We just need to find a boat."

"Hannah," her father said with a frown. "I told you I'd think on it."

"Well, you don't have that much time. You said entries close in a few days. What do you think, Uncle Joe?"

He grinned with approval. "I like it."

"I haven't agreed to anything," her father interrupted. "And that boat I built for the Blackthornes is probably unbeatable."

"I'm sure it's amazing," she said. "But it still needs a sailor, and you are the best there is."

"She's right about that," Joe said. "What about Howard Palmer's boat?"

"I'm sure he's racing it."

"Nope. His wife made him go on an African safari with his in-laws. He left two days ago and won't be back until June."

"Is that a possibility, Dad? Is his boat a good fit?"

"He's never won with it," her father replied. "But he's not the best racer, either."

"I think you should do it, Frank," Joe said. "After the way

the Blackthornes treated you, if nothing else, you can take that trophy they love so much."

"To be fair, Devlin has treated me well," Frank said. "It's his father I have a problem with."

"Well, you know how much Graham loves to get in the winning race photos, even when he's never actually on the boat," Joe reminded her father. "I'll text Palmer now and ask him if his boat is available."

"He'll have to agree to let me fix it up," Frank said. "I'm not going to race if I have no chance of winning."

"I'm sure he'll be thrilled to have you work on his boat."

She smiled at her dad as Joe typed out a text. "This will be good," she assured him. "We haven't sailed together in a long time."

Her dad nodded, but she could see indecision in his eyes. "It's not that I don't want to sail with you, Hannah; it's more complicated than that. I'm not a Blackthorne, but I've built their business and their boats. I've always been a loyal man."

"You have, but Graham hasn't shown you the same loyalty."

"Already got an answer," Joe interjected, an excited gleam in his eyes. "Palmer said yes. He didn't have to think about it for a second. You've got yourself a boat, Frank, and you can do whatever you want to it. Oh, and he says you better win."

"We will," she said confidently.

Her dad reluctantly smiled. "Now I know what it feels like to be steamrolled."

Despite his words, she saw a new light in his eyes. He didn't look nearly as unhappy or defeated as he'd been a few minutes earlier. In fact, he picked up his spoon and slid it into his chowder, as if he'd suddenly found his appetite.

"You came at the perfect time, Uncle Joe," she said.

He gave her a warm look of understanding. "I think you did, too, Hannah."

CHAPTER THREE

NOT HANNAH, Devlin thought with an inward groan as he made his way into the Vault with his brothers, Ross and Logan. He'd been hoping to avoid her as long as possible. But there she was with her pretty blonde hair falling softly down her back. As she turned her head, and her blue-eyed gaze connected with his, she frowned, losing the sparkle in her eyes.

He shouldn't care that she didn't like him. It wasn't as if they'd had a relationship before this. But it still bothered him. He didn't like the position his father had put him in, and he had every intention of making everything right for Frank, but after what had happened with his parents tonight, that might take a little longer than he'd hoped. He needed Frank to hang on, and he needed Hannah to understand that while he might be a Blackthorne, he was not as heartless as she thought.

"Why don't you guys get a table? I'll be over in a minute," he told his brothers. "I need to talk to someone." He headed across the room and slid into the empty chair between Hannah and her father.

"I don't think we invited you to sit down," Frank said shortly, giving him a grim look.

"I knew you were about to," he lied, offering them both a smile that was not reciprocated by either one.

"Unless you're here to tell us that my father is rehired, I don't think we have anything to say to you," Hannah said.

"Unfortunately, I was unable to speak to my dad tonight. The party took a surprising turn, and to be honest, my father has an even bigger problem to deal with now. I know you won't want to hear this, but I need you to give me a few days to talk to him, to get him to come around."

"What happened tonight?" Frank asked.

"My mother walked out of her birthday party. She announced she was leaving my dad, packed a suitcase and took off. I have no idea where she went."

While Hannah let out a gasp of surprise, Frank didn't seem to be as stunned as he would have expected.

"I can't believe she actually did it," Frank muttered.

His gut twisted. "You knew she was thinking about leaving my father?"

"I wouldn't say that. But I knew she was unhappy, that she was trying to get Graham to take more time off. She wanted him to commit to spending more than the summer here. She thought if she could get him out of Boston, he'd be different, less absorbed with work," Frank said.

"When did she tell you that?"

Frank shrugged. "She has said it a few times over the past year, but we had coffee about a week ago, and she was more upset than I'd ever seen her. I told Graham if he didn't start paying attention to his wife, he was going to lose her, but he didn't want to listen to me. He thinks he knows everything. He's always right, and everyone else is always wrong."

He suddenly realized what had precipitated Frank's firing. "You should have told me about this conversation."

"It wasn't my place to tell you. And I wouldn't have said anything to Graham if he hadn't demanded to know what I was talking to Claire about. But, as usual, your father didn't want to hear criticism. I can't believe she actually left him. But I guess she felt she needed to make a big statement to get Graham's attention."

"She certainly did that. She was different tonight. She was angry, but she was also determined."

"Well, she deserves to be happy as much as your father does. But I'm sure they'll work it out." Frank put his napkin on the table. "I need some air. Hannah, I'm going to walk home. You bring the car when you're ready. I'll see you back at the house."

"Wait. I'll come with you," Hannah said. "I'll just pay the bill."

"I wouldn't mind some time to myself." Frank waved her back into her seat. "Have another drink. Come home whenever you want."

Hannah didn't look thrilled with her father for abandoning her, but she let him go.

"I told you there was something personal between our fathers, and that's why your dad was fired," he said.

"Yes, you said I didn't know everything. Apparently, neither did you."

"You're right." He ran a hand through his hair. "I certainly had no idea my mom was thinking about leaving my dad. They've been married for thirty-seven years."

"You didn't know they were having problems?"

"No. I thought she was a little depressed, but I figured it was about turning sixty, getting older. I guess I wasn't paying enough attention." He felt a rush of guilt that he'd put off one-on-one time with his mom, because he'd been so busy getting the boat ready to race. "But your father was there for her, and she confided in him. I didn't realize they were close enough for that kind of conversation. But obviously they had a deep enough relationship to speak about extremely personal matters."

Hannah's gaze narrowed. "Are you accusing my father of

something? Because my dad would not mess around with a married woman, especially not the wife of his boss. That's insane."

"Maybe, but if my father thought differently, then that would have been a damn good reason for him to fire Frank."

"He fired my dad because he didn't like the message, so he wanted to kill the messenger."

He really wanted to believe that was true.

"We have to clear this up, Devlin," Hannah continued. "I won't have you suggesting that my father was cheating with your mother."

"I am definitely not suggesting that to anyone," he snapped back. "God, that's the last thing I would do. We don't need any more gossip or rumors about secrets."

"Okay then, good."

"You do realize now that there's no way you or I can change this situation. It's between Frank and my dad. They have to work this out."

"That's not true. You can still fight for my dad's job. Just because he listened to your mom and made the mistake of actually telling your dad a truth he didn't want to hear doesn't mean he should lose his livelihood. He built the Boatworks to what it is today. You've only been working there what—five years? My dad has been there thirty. You owe him a lot."

"God, you're stubborn," he said, both impressed and a little unnerved by the intensity in her expression.

"I fight for the people I love. And if you care about my dad at all, you should fight for him, too, because you know it's the right thing to do."

He wished he could say she was wrong, but she wasn't. "I will fight for Frank, Hannah. But I need to give my father a little time to regroup."

"You better not wait too long, or you'll be watching my dad cross the finish line in front of you."

He frowned at her words. "What are you talking about?"

"My dad will not sit out the race on Memorial Day week-end. I'm going to help him win the trophy for himself this time and not for the Blackthornes."

He was shocked at her words. He hadn't really thought about losing Frank for the race, because he'd been sure that Frank would be back to work before then. "You and Frank are going to race against me?"

"You and whoever else you get on your boat," she said, a fighting light in her blue eyes.

"What boat will you be racing?"

"You'll see," she said vaguely.

He wondered what boat Frank could possibly lay his hands on two weeks before the race. But with his connections, he could probably find one. Anger and disappointment ran through him. He felt pissed off at everyone—his father for being an ass, his mother for leaving without any real explanation, Frank for giving up so soon, and especially Hannah, who was looking quite proud of herself.

He could appreciate her defense of her father, but she was stirring up problems that didn't have to be there. If his father found out Frank was racing a competitive boat, that would make it even more difficult for him to get Frank rehired. "Why don't you take a breath, Hannah? You're getting so far down the road that there will be a point where there's no coming back."

"Come back from what? My dad has no job and has been fired after thirty years of loyal service. How much worse could things get?"

"You could make it impossible for him to get rehired."

"By racing against you? Would you be that petty?"

"Not me, but…"

"I'm really beginning to dislike your dad."

He could see why she would. "He's not a bad guy. He has a lot of good traits, in fact. He can actually be very generous."

"Not that I've seen. And I really wish everyone would stop telling me to breathe," she added grumpily.

"You're moving too fast for your father, too, aren't you?"

"I thought you and my dad liked speed," she countered.

"On the ocean, we do."

"Not on land?"

"That depends. And sometimes it's better to go slow," he couldn't help adding.

She flushed a little at his words, and he found himself entranced by that wash of red through her cheeks, as well as the uncomfortable sparkle in her eyes. He hadn't felt this charged up in a while. Fighting with Hannah was probably more fun than it should be. And he was amused that he'd finally found a way to apparently leave her speechless.

Fortunately for Hannah, a waitress stopped by their table. Shelby was an attractive redhead in her early twenties, the daughter of one of his employees, and he'd known her since she was about ten.

"Hi, Devlin. How are you?" she asked, setting two glasses of Blackthorne Gold whiskey on the table. "Your brothers sent this over."

He turned his head to see Ross and Logan looking on with speculative gleams in their eyes.

"You can take mine back," Hannah told Shelby, handing her the glass. "I'll have a chardonnay."

"Are you sure? This is top of the line," Shelby said.

"I'm positive," Hannah said definitively. "And you can bring the bill when you come back."

"All right."

"You can leave the whisky for me," he told Shelby. "I have a feeling I'll need a second drink sooner rather than later."

She set the glass down in front of him. "You got it."

"Not a whisky drinker?" he asked Hannah.

"Not really, but I'm also not interested in drinking

anything that comes out of a bottle with a Blackthorne label on it."

"Yet you're here in the Vault, which is owned by my family."

"I know," she said with a sigh. "My dad loves the chowder, and he said he wasn't letting you take anything else away from him. I would have preferred to go anywhere else."

"My family is not that bad. And until this week, your father was very happy with his job."

"Well, everything is different now, isn't it?"

"That's certainly true," he muttered.

Her expression softened. "I am sorry about your mom, Devlin. She was always very nice to me." She paused. "I actually know what it feels like to watch the end of a marriage. It sucks."

"It does suck. My parents have always been so strong together. I'm sure they disagree, but they always kept that away from us. They were all about being a united front. Apparently, that front was an illusion."

"Or perhaps your mother just got angry and needed to get away for a bit. Do you know where she went?"

"No idea, but I'm sure my father has someone looking for her." He paused, thinking about Hannah's family. "How did it happen between your parents? Did you know a divorce was coming?"

"In retrospect—yes. They fought a lot. But I didn't want to believe it would actually happen. It's actually ironic to think my dad told your father to stop working so much and try to save his marriage, when he refused to do that for my mother or for me."

"Was that the main problem between them?"

"It was certainly one of the biggest ones." She paused as Shelby brought her wine and the bill. "Thanks," she said to the waitress.

Shelby nodded and moved on to the next table.

"Your dad loves to work," he commented. "Boats are his passion."

"I know," she said, sipping her wine. "I think he also felt that long hours were expected. Before you were at the Boatworks, your father was in charge and then that other guy—what was his name?"

"Bill Walker?"

"Yes. He was always telling my dad that he needed him in earlier and earlier and sometimes on the weekends. He'd also ask him to travel to inspect some boat or hand-deliver a yacht. It drove my mom crazy that my dad could never say no."

"Maybe he didn't want to say no."

"I'm sure he didn't. As you said, he loves to work. Which is why I'm so worried about him now. His job has been his whole life. He lost everything else."

He thought about that, wondering if he wasn't going down the same path as Frank, maybe even his father...

That was a disturbing thought. The last person he had ever wanted to be was his dad.

"But it wasn't all about my father's job," Hannah continued. "I didn't realize this until I was an adult, but my mom didn't just want my dad to spend more time with her; she wanted her own dream. And she couldn't have it in this small town."

"The dream of real estate? They sell houses here."

"They do, but I think she was in loyal wife mode back then. She didn't want to leave me with a sitter while they were both working. Once we left, she had no choice. She had to make it on her own. Leaving my dad's shadow, moving away from his needs, gave her the opportunity to find herself. Over the last ten years, she has built one of the most successful real estate companies in Austin."

"So, the split was good for her."

"Yes. It was good for her and good for him—me, not so

much. I still miss the family I once had, being able to be together, especially on holidays or birthdays. As a kid, it was hard to split time, and as an adult, I've seen less and less of my father. Divorce is really hard on kids." She paused. "But your parents will probably get back together. This is just a fight."

"I hope so. It's difficult to see either one without the other. I really thought they were true partners in every sense of the word. When my dad is with my mom, he's different. He's kinder, softer, more generous, more attentive. She balances him out."

"What does he do for her?"

He frowned at the question, then tossed back the rest of his whisky, letting the warm, smooth slide of liquid take away some of the guilt he felt for never asking that question himself, for possibly taking his mom for granted, the way apparently everyone else in the family had done.

"My dad has given her a great life," he said finally. "They've built an incredible family and legacy together."

"Maybe she wants something of her own."

"Like your mom?"

Hannah shrugged. "Possibly."

"That's actually exactly what she said and in a very dramatic fashion, which was even more strange, because she was never one to air any family laundry in public. But she gave it to my father in front of their friends and even some business associates. She told him off in very firm terms, saying she'd given her life for him. She even mentioned something about keeping his secret, whatever that is."

"That's an odd thing to say."

"I thought so, too." He picked up the second glass of whisky and drank it halfway down. He was starting to get a nice buzz going, which was probably a bad idea, because watching Hannah through a blurred whisky gaze was bringing all kinds of foolish thoughts into his head.

"Is that Logan?" Hannah asked, tipping her head toward his brothers, who were still watching them with considerable interest.

"Yes, and my brother, Ross."

"I remember Logan. He was the closest in age to me and so popular. Every girl wanted to date him. When I'd visit in the summers, my friends were always trying to find ways to accidentally run into him."

He smiled. "Logan has never had any shortage of girls after him."

"The same is true for you and the rest of your tribe. Are any of your brothers or cousins married?"

"Not yet."

"Do most of them live in Boston?"

"We're all spread out. I'm the only one who lives full-time in King Harbor. My cousins, Phillip, Jason, and Brock are in DC, LA, and Boston respectively. My brother Trey is also in Boston, while Ross is in Kentucky, and Logan jumps around from place to place."

"Why did you choose to live here?"

"The sea," he said with a simple shrug. "There's nowhere else I'd rather be."

"Is there a woman in your life?"

"Only one who's annoying the hell out of me right now."

She rolled her eyes. "Very funny."

"What about you? I don't see a ring on your finger."

She shifted in her seat, an uncomfortable look entering her eyes. "There's no ring now."

"You were engaged?" he asked in surprise. "I'm surprised I never heard that."

"Why would you have heard it?"

"Frank talks about you sometimes, but he didn't tell me you were engaged."

"He didn't know. I was going to tell him, but it ended before I had a chance."

"That sounds like a very short engagement."

"Three days. The story I would have to tell is actually longer than the engagement."

"I'd like to hear it."

She finished her drink. "Unfortunately, I'm out of wine."

"I could get you another glass."

"Not a good idea."

"Why not? Are you afraid you might start to like me?" he challenged, the whisky probably making him a little too reckless. "That the sparks between us aren't just coming from anger?"

"I don't know what you're talking about," she denied, but he could see the glitter of awareness in her eyes. "We have never had any sparks."

"Not before now," he agreed.

"I'm not looking for another relationship."

"Who said anything about a relationship?"

"You're drunk."

"Not yet."

She got to her feet. "Goodnight, Devlin."

He watched her walk out of the pub with mixed emotions, but he settled on the one that made the most sense—relief. He should be happy she was gone, because he'd been sailing into dangerous water, and on any other night he would have turned around a long time ago.

Getting up, he headed across the room and joined his brothers, who were eager to grill him.

"Was that Hannah Reid?" Logan asked.

"It was."

"I thought that might be her," he continued. "I haven't seen her in years, but she looks good."

"Really good," Ross put in with a grin. "However, she didn't look like she was buying what you were selling."

"She's angry. Dad fired Frank three days ago."

"No way. Why?" Ross asked in surprise. "Frank has been at the Boatworks forever."

"Well, I didn't find out until tonight that Frank apparently told Dad that he'd better shape up or he would lose Mom. Dad didn't appreciate his suggestion and fired him."

"Frank knew Mom was unhappy?" Ross asked, his gaze narrowing. "Did he give you more information?"

"No. He said he'd had coffee with Mom a week ago and she'd mentioned her frustration with Dad always putting work ahead of the family. Mom's anger has been simmering for at least a week. I think her birthday put her over the edge."

"Did he mention anything about a secret?" Logan asked curiously.

"Nope. I don't know what that was about, but I think it's clear Mom left Dad because he works all the time."

"Maybe that should be a cautionary tale for others in our family," Ross suggested. "Brock, Trey, Jason…they all spend way too much time at work."

"We're probably all guilty of that," he muttered. He'd certainly immersed himself in work the last several years. In fact, it was the work that had kept him sane, given him a purpose, when he'd been floundering.

But was he turning into Frank or his father? That was an uncomfortable thought.

"How long will Hannah be in town?" Logan asked.

"At least until after the Memorial Day race. She and Frank are going to find another boat and race against me."

"No way. You always race with Frank."

"Not this year. I need a partner. Either one of you want to volunteer?"

"Sorry, I have to get back to Kentucky," Ross said. "And I'm better in a fast car than a fast boat."

That was certainly true. Ross spent his time racing stock cars.

"I won't be here for Memorial Day," Logan said. "I have to get back to Boston."

"Well, hopefully someone will be around."

Ross gave him an evil grin. "You could always ask Dad."

"He hasn't raced since Uncle Mark died. I've asked him before, and he always says no." It bothered him more than a little that his father had never wanted to share in that part of his life, but he supposed he could understand that there were some painful memories involved. His uncle, his father's only sibling, had died in a tragic plane crash and it had been a huge loss in his dad's life.

"Maybe Dad will change his mind this year, if he has incentive. He is not going to want his boat to lose to the man he just fired," Ross pointed out.

"You're right." His dad would absolutely hate losing to Frank. Maybe he could get his father on board this year. *But did he really want him? Would the dream of racing with his dad turn out to be a nightmare?*

CHAPTER FOUR

HANNAH MADE breakfast Sunday morning feeling grumpy and annoyed, not just with Devlin for putting crazy ideas in her head, but also with herself for actually thinking about how much fun it might be to mess around with Devlin.

As a teenager, she'd had a crush on Devlin, because he was the Blackthorne who liked boats as much as she did. And his sunburned grin, charming swagger, and wild, wind-blown hair had always created a lot of awkward and uncomfortable feelings within her.

He'd created those same feelings last night when he'd spoken so bluntly about the sparks between them. She'd thought those sparks had all been on her side, remnants from her teenage years, but, no, Devlin had felt them, too. And there was a part of her that really liked the fact that he found her attractive now.

On the other hand, he'd had quite a bit to drink and his mom had just left his dad. He was obviously on an emotional roller coaster. She didn't want to be anyone's stress release, even if it would no doubt be a hell of a lot of fun. And she hadn't had a lot of that kind of fun in a long time. She had to admit that Devlin's interest was a salve to her bruised heart.

Losing Gary to his ex had brought all her insecurities to the forefront, and she was still trying to believe in herself again.

But Devlin had stood by while his father had fired her dad, and she couldn't forget that. She also couldn't forget that she would only be in town a few weeks, and that if her dream came true of racing with her father, that Devlin would be her biggest competitor.

It was all too messy and complicated. She needed to stay away from Devlin.

She just wished it was a little easier to stop thinking about him.

Cracking eggs into the skillet, she forced herself to concentrate on breakfast. She'd almost finished the veggie scramble when her dad walked into the kitchen. She hadn't talked to him since he'd left the pub the night before. When she'd gotten home, he'd been in his bedroom with the door closed.

But he looked brighter and more energetic this morning. He'd also shaved off the scraggly beard he'd been wearing the past two days.

"Perfect timing," she told him. "I have breakfast ready."

"You're spoiling me. And that looks better than the breakfasts you used to make me."

"You mean my special mix of chocolate puffs and wheat crisps didn't do it for you?" she asked with a laugh.

He smiled back at her. "Not quite. I was never as big a fan of cereal as you were."

"Well, sit down and we'll eat." She took their plates to the table and sat down across from him.

"This is excellent," he said, digging into his eggs. "Healthy, too. I can see your mom has rubbed off on you."

"Yes. I haven't been able to adopt her vegan lifestyle, but I do eat a lot more vegetables than I ever thought I would."

"Good for you."

"Have you thought any more about the race? About Howard Palmer's boat?"

"I have thought about it, and if you want, we can take a look at the boat after breakfast."

Her heart leapt with excitement. "Really?"

"I'm still not committing to race," he warned her. "I need to see the *Daisy Mae* again before I make a final decision."

"Understood." She hesitated. "I know I shouldn't have, but I did mention to Devlin that we might race against him."

"Hannah! You shouldn't have said anything yet."

"It just came out. I'm sorry. But in case you were wondering, he looked a little worried."

Her father's lips tightened. "What else did you talk about?"

"Not much really." She wasn't about to tell her dad that Devlin had hit on her. "He was pretty shaken about his mom leaving. Apparently, when she left the house, she also said something about keeping Graham's secrets, and no one knows what she meant. Do you know?" she asked curiously.

"No idea. But that's between Graham and Claire."

"Do you think you should talk to Graham again?" she asked tentatively. "Maybe you could work out the problems between you. After what happened with Claire, he might now realize that you were just trying to warn him."

"I doubt it," her dad said shortly, making her wonder if more had gone down between him and Graham than just some pointed advice.

"Does that mean you don't want your job back?"

"Not at all. But I'm not going to beg for it. The Black-thornes don't have the market on pride. I have nothing to apologize for. They need to come to me with not only my job but a better offer before I'd consider going back."

"And if they don't, then what?"

"Then I'll figure something else out. It's not your problem,

Hannah. I appreciate your concern. But I've been taking care of myself a long time."

"I just want to help."

"You've always wanted to help fix things that are broken, but some things are not yours to fix."

"You said that to me a long time ago, when you and Mom split up."

He nodded, his gaze somber. "I needed you to let go of a dream that wasn't going to come true."

It had taken her years to let go of that dream. She did tend to hang on too long, trying to fix problems that weren't always hers to fix. Maybe she was doing the same thing now. She just had a hard time standing by and doing nothing when people she loved were hurting.

Deciding to focus on the one action her father was still considering, she said, "I'll take a shower and then we can go look at Howard's boat."

"All right. And, Hannah, don't think I don't appreciate you, because I do."

She gave him a smile. "I know I can push hard. It's because I love you."

"I love you, too, and sometimes I can use a hard push. I know I haven't been the perfect dad."

"I was never looking for perfect. I just wanted you in my life."

"I'm glad you're here now."

"Me, too. Let's go get ourselves a boat."

He laughed. "Don't get too far ahead, Hannah. I know Howard Palmer well, and I'm betting that boat hasn't been maintained very well the past several years."

"Well, I know you, and you can fix anything."

Sunday morning, Devlin found his dad sitting at the patio

table in front of an untouched breakfast, his gaze on the newspaper in front of him. While his father could be technologically advanced at work, when it came to books and the news, he always preferred print.

He slid into the seat across from him, noting his father's haggard expression, the deep lines around his eyes and mouth that seemed more pronounced this morning. He usually had a good tan going, but today his skin was pale. He even seemed to have picked up a few more gray hairs since last night.

"I'm not in the mood to talk, Devlin," his dad said, not bothering to raise his gaze from the newspaper.

"Is that why you're sitting here alone?"

"Yes." His father finally looked at him. "Your brothers and cousins are respecting my choice to be alone. Why can't you?"

"I'm sorry about what happened. Do you know where Mom is?"

"Not yet, but I will shortly."

"Have you spoken to her?"

"No. Your mother made it clear that she wasn't interested in a conversation. When she is, we'll talk."

"When you figure out where she is, maybe you should go to her and show her that you want to talk," he said, choosing his words carefully. "It sounded like she felt taken for granted."

"Which is ridiculous. I have taken care of her to the best of my ability my entire life."

"I don't think she was talking about being taken care of. She wants to spend more time with you."

His father sent him a warning look. "Don't get in the middle of this, Devlin. It's not your business."

"She's my mother."

"And she's my wife. When you're married, you'll understand that that relationship doesn't involve your children."

"Okay," he said, blowing out a breath. "Then let's talk about Frank."

"I'm not hiring him back."

"Then I will. He's in the middle of a huge design project, not to mention the other boats in production. I also need him for the race. It's our opportunity to show off the *Wind Warrior*. We'll get double the price if we win."

"Find someone else to race with you."

"There's no one else as good as Frank."

"Don't be ridiculous. Of course there is."

"Putting the race aside, Frank's job at the Boatworks is too important to let an emotional decision get in the way of business."

His father's eyes filled with anger. "Emotional decision?"

"Yes," he said flatly. "Frank told me that the two of you spoke about Mom's unhappiness and that you didn't like the message he was giving you, so you fired him."

"He had no right getting into my business."

"Is it possible he was trying to help you? After all, Mom did leave."

Fire entered his dad's gaze, and Devlin sucked in a breath, knowing he was probably crossing a line he shouldn't cross, but it was too late to take back his words.

"I told you to stay out of this, Devlin."

"You put me in the middle of it. Is there something I don't know?" He licked his lips. "I don't want to ask this, but—"

"Then don't," his dad said, cutting him off.

"You can't think there's anything between Mom and Frank. She would never do that to you, and neither would Frank. He's an honorable man."

"Devlin, stop. Frank is done," his father said, shoving back his chair so hard that it fell over when he stood up. "If you hire him back, I swear to God I'll shut the Boatworks down. Do you understand me?"

He understood a lot of things, including the fact that his

father wasn't just angry, he was in pain. He could see it in his eyes, hear it in the ragged edges of his voice. He should have waited to have this conversation. "I understand."

His father brushed past him and stomped into the house.

He stood up and moved over to the rail, looking out over the ocean. He needed to be on the sea. It was the one place he could count on to find his center, his calm. He'd planned on taking the boat out tomorrow for a test run, but maybe today would be good. There was a nice breeze and plenty of sunshine, which would be a good contrast to the shadows filling his soul. His family was breaking apart, and he didn't know how to stop it.

"Devlin?"

He turned around at the sound of Trey's voice. His brother was dressed more casually this morning in jeans and a long-sleeved knit shirt. "Good morning."

"Did you just talk to Dad?" Trey asked, concern in his eyes. "He walked past me looking like he was about to explode."

"Unfortunately, yes."

"Did he have anything to say?"

"No. He shut me down. His damn pride always gets in the way."

"He may be proud, but he's also rattled. This has completely spun his world upside down."

"I know, and I made things worse. I asked him to hire Frank back. That set him off like a Fourth of July rocket."

Trey nodded. "I saw Ross earlier. He told me that Frank tried to warn Dad that Mom was unhappy."

"And Dad now thinks that there was something going on between Frank and Mom."

"No way," Trey said dismissively. "That's crazy. Mom would never cheat on Dad."

"I don't believe she would, either, but Dad can't stand the fact that she confided in Frank. He's so jealous he can't see that the real problem is him. Mom was very clear about why she was leaving."

"She was, and I'm sorry for my part in what happened. I had no idea she'd react so strongly to the McKinney brothers showing up at her party."

"I wouldn't have anticipated that, either. This isn't on you, Trey; it's on Dad."

"I just wish it hadn't happened."

"Are you going to stick around for a while? I'm thinking about taking the new boat out for a test run this afternoon. You could come with me."

"I wish I could, but I need to get back to Boston. We'll talk soon."

"Sure."

"And Devlin, maybe let this Frank business settle for a while. I know you need Frank working for you, but the timing is bad."

"I could lose him, Trey. There are any number of firms who would love to snap him up."

"Not here in Maine, and he has never wanted to live anywhere else."

"That could change."

"Is Frank pushing you to hire him back?"

"Actually, he hasn't said much, but his daughter is another story."

"Little Hannah?"

"Not so little anymore," he returned, Hannah's beautiful image flashing in front of his eyes. "She's a grown woman and a spitfire. She has been all over me about our very poor treatment of her father, our most loyal employee, and I can't say she's wrong. The other employees are unhappy with the situation as well. With Hannah stirring up trouble, I could have a mutiny on my hands if this doesn't end soon."

"Who knew the boat business could be so dramatic?"

Trey said lightly. "You'll figure things out, and I think both Mom and Dad will come to their senses."

"Hopefully before my entire company collapses."

"You can head that off. Sweet-talk the spitfire—use that old Devlin charm," Trey said, slapping him on the shoulder. "Ross mentioned that Hannah is a beautiful woman now. He said you two had a long conversation last night."

"She is very attractive, yes. But it will take more than charm to get Hannah off my back," he said dryly.

"Maybe you should get her on her back," Trey joked.

He shook his head. "Go to Boston; you are no help."

As his brother left, he couldn't help picturing Hannah on her back in the middle of his bed. And his morning just got a little better.

CHAPTER FIVE

Hannah and her father spent an hour examining every nook and cranny of the *Daisy Mae*. Her fear that her father would decide against sailing the boat grew with each passing minute. She wanted to ask him for an answer, but she was afraid if she pushed too soon, he'd say no.

She had to admit that the sailboat had seen better days, and she was starting to have her own doubts as to whether they could win with it. But she'd rather try with this boat than give up altogether, and she doubted they could find another boat that would be in better condition this close to the race.

"Well?" she asked, unable to keep the impatient note out of her voice. "What do you think, Dad?"

He gave her a somewhat unhappy look. "I think I've spent the past year building the *Wind Warrior*, and I sure wish I could race her."

"That's not an option at the moment. It's not just about the boat, right? It's also about the crew, too. We can beat Devlin and whoever he gets to go with him," she said confidently.

"Devlin is a very skilled racer, Hannah. Don't underestimate him."

"I'm not underestimating him, but I know you are better than him."

He smiled. "Trying to flatter me into a yes?"

"I mean every word. I think it's time the Reids showed the Blackthornes they aren't the only ones who can win."

"Well, when you put it like that…I'm in. Let's race together."

A wave of pleasure ran through her. "Great. This will be fun, Dad."

"More fun if we win."

"That's the plan."

"I need to get to work on this boat. It could take several days to get her ready to go in the water."

"I can help."

"Not today. I appreciate the offer, but I need to do this part on my own. I need to spend some time on the details, and you're not particularly patient when I'm scoping things out."

"Guilty," she admitted.

"It's a nice day. Why don't you go out and meet up with some of your friends?"

"I don't have any friends left around here."

"You don't? You used to have so many girlfriends to see in the summers."

"Which was a long time ago."

"Not that long."

"True. Maybe I'll walk down to the harbor and see if there is anyone at the Yacht Club who can take our entry fee."

"Good idea. Look for Grace Varney. She's in charge of the entries."

"Mrs. Varney is in charge? Her daughter Jessica was one of my good friends in elementary school."

"Well, Jessica is still in town. See, you do have some friends here."

"I haven't seen her in years."

"If you want to see her again, she works at the distillery giving tours."

"Another Blackthorne employee," she said with a sigh.

"In this town, you'd be hard-pressed to find too many people who don't collect a paycheck from the Blackthornes. Anyway, go on, get out of here. If you want to take my truck…"

"No. You might need it to run out and pick up supplies and you know I enjoy walking. I'll see you later."

She left the Palmers' boathouse and headed into town. The harbor was only about a mile and a half away, and it was a beautiful day. No clouds, only bright sunshine, and a crisp ocean breeze. It was too bad the *Daisy Mae* needed work, because it was a great day for a sail. They could have taken her out on the water and seen what she could do. But as her father would say, that would be putting the cart before the horse. At some point in her life, she really did need to learn patience.

As she strolled through the streets of her childhood, warm memories ran through her. She'd been happy growing up in King Harbor. She'd loved riding bikes with her friends, hanging out at the beaches, going out on boats whenever she got a chance. She'd loved running into neighbors every time they went to the market or out to eat. She'd always felt like she was part of a big family and that there were many people who cared about her.

That had all changed when she was thirteen, when her mother had moved them both to Texas. While she'd come to love Austin, she'd missed the ocean and the King Harbor community. She'd come back in the summers, but it had never been the same. For one thing, summers in the small coastal town were different than the rest of the year. From Memorial Day to Labor Day, the population quadrupled in size and the lavish estates dotting the shoreline were filled with their wealthy homeowners and their friends and family.

The Blackthornes had been part of the summer crowd, showing up on Memorial Day weekend for the boat races and then reappearing in June when the kids would be out of school.

Their King Harbor businesses, the Boatworks, the distillery and the Vault to name a few, ran all year round, but it was the local employees who mostly kept them going. She'd always thought the Blackthornes appreciated their managers—until now. Frowning, she pushed that annoying thought out of her head. There was nothing she could do about that situation at the moment, but her dad had a new goal, and hopefully the boat race would not only distract him from his problems but would also bring them closer together.

She'd missed him the last few years when their visits had dwindled to meeting up for a night somewhere at Christmas or New Year's and the occasional weekend, usually at some location where her father was delivering a boat. Now, she had at least a couple of weeks to reconnect.

As she neared the harbor, she could see boats motoring in and out of their slips, and out on the water were more than a few brightly colored sails. She wondered if Devlin was out on the ocean today, or if he was dealing with a whisky hangover. She suspected he and his brothers had had a few more drinks after she'd left the Vault. It had definitely been the night for it.

She crossed the street in front of the King Harbor Yacht Club, which was housed in a two-story white stucco building, with massive floor-to-ceiling windows overlooking the harbor. The Yacht Club had been founded by Devlin's grandfather—Graham the first. He'd also been the one to start the Boatworks. Devlin's father, Graham the second, and his Uncle Mark had worked at the Boatworks during the summers when they were in high school. But Mark had gone on to become a lawyer and Graham had become more interested in expanding Blackthorne Enterprises to encompass a number of different businesses, each adding more and more to the bottom line.

While Devlin had worked at the Boatworks during the summer, he had become its manager five years ago when the former manager, Bill Walker, had retired. According to her dad, Devlin had done a great job building the business and the brand of Blackthorne boats, but sometimes she thought her father gave him too much credit. But that was her dad; he'd always been more comfortable behind the scenes, and with Devlin in charge, her father had been able to concentrate on what he liked most—design and construction.

She couldn't imagine what Devlin would do without her dad's creativity and expertise, but he was going to find out. Just like he would find out how it felt to lose to her father instead of win with him.

She entered the building with an eager step, moving past the restaurant and bar, which were busy with Sunday brunch, and jogging up the stairs to the administrative offices. In the reception area, she was greeted with the warm brown eyes of Grace Varney.

"Mrs. Varney?"

"Oh, my goodness—Hannah. You're back." Grace got to her feet and came around the counter to give her a hug. "How are you?"

"I'm very well, thanks. And you?"

"I'm great. Your father must be over the moon that you're home. Although, you probably don't still think of King Harbor as home, but we still think of you as one of us. Jessica would love to see you. How long will you be in town?"

"Probably until Memorial Day."

"You know what—we're having a birthday party for Jessica on Wednesday night in the banquet room here. It starts at seven. Why don't you come by?"

"I wouldn't want to intrude," she said hesitantly.

"You would not be intruding. You know how parties are at

our house—the more the merrier. Please say you'll come. I won't take no for an answer."

She laughed. "Then I'll say yes. It sounds like fun."

"Wonderful. Now what can I do for you?"

"My dad and I have decided to race together Memorial Day weekend."

"Really?" Grace asked in surprise. "But won't Frank be on the Blackthorne boat with Devlin? They're the odds-on favorite to win again this year."

"My father and I will actually be racing on another boat."

"Another boat? But why? Your father builds the Blackthorne boats. And from what I hear, the *Wind Warrior* is top of the line."

"That's all true, but this year will be different," she said vaguely, quite sure her father didn't want her talking about the termination of his employment. Hopefully, he'd be back at his job before anyone heard about it. "Can we still enter?"

"Of course." Grace moved back around the counter, then paused, speculation in her eyes. "I've heard a few rumors about the Blackthornes letting Frank go, but I don't want to believe they are true."

"It's a complicated situation. I don't think my dad wants me talking about it."

"Well, I hope they work it out."

"Me, too, but in the meantime, I'm looking forward to racing with my dad."

Grace pulled a paper out of the file folder. "Here's the entry form. Fill it out, pay the fee and you're set."

"Great."

She spent a few minutes filling out the form, then handed over her credit card. While Grace completed the transaction, her gaze moved toward the window overlooking the docks. She stiffened when she saw Devlin talking to another man. He wore faded jeans and a T-shirt that clung to his broad shoulders, and her stomach did a little flip-flop at the sight of him.

Devlin laughed at something the other man said, then gave a wave and headed down the ramp. *Was he going for a sail? Maybe taking out the Wind Warrior for a test run?* Her father had mentioned that they'd planned on putting the boat in the water this weekend.

After taking her receipt from Grace, she headed back down the stairs and outside. Instead of returning to the Palmer's boathouse, she moved around the building. If Devlin had the *Wind Warrior* in a slip, she'd like to take a closer look. She told herself she was just sizing up the competition; it had nothing to do with wanting to see Devlin again. But that was too big of a lie for even her to believe.

She found Devlin on the deck of a sleek and sophisticated boat. When he saw her, he gave her a sexy grin. "Well, look who's here."

"I was at the Yacht Club signing up for the race."

"I guess your dad found a boat."

"Yes. I hope you won't be too disappointed with second place."

He laughed. "You're very confident, Hannah."

"Something wrong with that?"

"Not at all. Whose boat will you be sailing?"

"Not your business."

"I'll find out soon enough."

"Then that's when you'll find out." She didn't particularly want to hear his opinion of the *Daisy Mae's* chances against the *Wind Warrior*, because her dad was right. This boat would be tough to beat. It had all the bells and whistles anyone could want, and probably some features that no one but her dad and Devlin had thought about.

"Want to come aboard?" he asked.

"I should probably get back."

"You know you want to see the boat."

She hesitated, not liking the knowing gleam in his brown eyes, but he was right. "I'm a little curious," she admitted.

He extended his hand, and as she moved up the stairs, his warm fingers curling around hers, she felt a jolt of electricity run through her. When she hit the deck, she stepped away as quickly as she could, trying to calm her suddenly racing heart.

Devlin gave her a look that told her he knew exactly how she was feeling.

She turned her gaze away from him, trying to focus on the boat. The *Wind Warrior* was branded as a B40, referencing the Blackthorne brand and the forty-foot size. Even on first glance, it was easy to see that every detail was designed to provide both comfort in cruising and speed in racing.

The cockpit was uncluttered, the large 48" wheel, allowing the helmsman and mainsheet trimmer to sit side-by-side upwind. The rigging was simple and clean, with lines leading to winches on either side of the companionway. The main sheet was double-ended with a winch on either side of the cockpit so that the mainsheet trimmer could sit outboard.

"What do you think?" he asked.

"She's very pretty."

"Yes, she is. Now, I need to see how fast she can fly."

"I should let you get to it."

"Why don't you come with me, Hannah?"

The invitation was both unexpected and very tempting. "Aren't you afraid I'll see too much, now that I'm your competition?"

"Since your father built every inch of this boat, there are no secrets. When's the last time you were out on the water?"

"Probably five years," she admitted.

"That sounds like a lifetime to me."

"It actually feels that way to me, too. I've been meaning to get back to King Harbor for a while, but I got busy with work, and I never seemed to find the time."

"Well, now is the perfect time for a sail. Are you really going to turn me down, Hannah?"

How on earth could she say no to the sexy lure of not only Devlin but also the ocean? "All right. I'll go," she said, hoping she wouldn't regret it.

"Great. It will give me a chance to see how good you are."

"So, you do have an ulterior motive." Now that he'd reminded her that her skills were about to be shown, she was plagued with doubts. She was rusty and if he saw that, it could give him an edge. Although, in reality, it was her father he had to beat. She'd be doing whatever her dad told her to do.

Devlin jumped off the boat, releasing the lines and then pushing off before he jumped back on board to take the helm.

As they motored their way through the harbor, she was surprised by how many boats were in port. "It's crowded," she commented.

"The racers come earlier and earlier every year. For this event, we already have a record number of boats competing. That's why I was wondering what boat your dad had found."

"Like I said, you'll have to keep wondering."

He grinned. "I hope it's not the *Daisy Mae*. I know Howard is in Africa right now. That old lady wouldn't be able to touch this girl."

"It's not just about the boat."

"That's what your father always tells me."

"It's true."

"Your dad is an incredible racer. His instincts are amazing."

"Getting nervous?"

"It will be a challenge," he admitted.

"Who will you race with?"

"I'm not sure yet. I'm hoping to get one of my brothers or cousins on board, but so far, they have all said no. They came for the party but left early today to get back to their lives."

"What are they all doing?" she asked curiously.

"My oldest brother Trey and my cousin Brock live and work in Boston. Trey is executive vice president of operations and Brock is senior vice president of brand management for Blackthorne Enterprises."

"That sounds very official."

"They are both following in my father's footsteps. My brother Ross is not. He races stock cars in Kentucky, although I think my dad is pressuring him to work in the distillery there."

"What about Logan?"

"He seems to be jumping around a lot. He's learning various parts of the business but hasn't committed yet to what he wants to do or where he wants to be. He still puts having a good time over just about everything else."

"That's the way I remember him. He was always a lot of fun. And your other two cousins?"

"Phillip lives in DC. He runs a non-profit org that sends kids who have suffered a tragic loss in their lives to camp."

"Like he and his brothers did when your aunt and uncle died."

He nodded, a somber look in his eyes. "That was a horrible time."

She was sorry she'd dragged him back to that memory. "And last but not least…"

His smile returned. "That would be Jason. He lives in LA and runs Blackthorne Entertainment. He is currently producing a detective TV series that just started airing. He's actually scouting locations for the second season here in King Harbor, but he says he can't commit to the race and that I'd be a fool to want him on the boat," he said dryly. "He knows his strengths and apparently doesn't feel that sailboat racing is one of them."

"That's honest. It would be cool to see the town on television."

"I'm not sure King Harbor is ready for the Hollywood crowd, but I suppose it would bring in more business, which is always good."

"True. It does sound like everyone in your family is too busy to sail with you, Devlin. What about your dad? Would you ever race with him?"

"He hasn't raced since my Uncle Mark died. Although, he might appreciate the incentive of beating your father."

"If he's on your boat, my dad will have even more incentive to beat you."

"Well, I wouldn't get too excited. I don't think my dad will get on this boat. He's never said yes to me before."

There was an odd note in Devlin's voice that made her curious. "Are you and your father close?"

He gave a short laugh. "No. We rarely see eye to eye on anything."

"Then how do you work for him?"

"We don't work together. I only agreed to run the Boatworks because he usually has nothing to do with it, but, as we both know now, your father's termination was not about the business." He paused. "I spoke to my dad again this morning, Hannah. He told me to stay out of it. I'm sorry, but at the moment there's nothing else I can do. My dad is reeling from my mom's abrupt departure, and your dad is tangled up in that."

"I know," she admitted. "I'm disappointed, but I understand that you're caught in the middle."

He flung her a quick look. "I'm glad. Your father might have better luck if he talks to my dad himself."

"He won't do that. He says he is not going to beg for his job when he didn't do anything wrong."

"Looks like we have a stalemate, at least for the moment. Why don't we forget about our obstinate parents for a while?"

"That sounds like a great idea." Turning her head, her gaze swept the shoreline, loving the sight of all the colorful houses tucked into the hills overlooking the water. "I always wanted to live in one of those homes."

"They're nice," he agreed.

"My mom used to take me to open houses on the weekends when we lived here. Even then she was fascinated with real estate, but, of course, we had no money to buy anything. And my dad was happy to live in the two-bedroom house three blocks away from the Boatworks that he lives in now."

"It is convenient."

"Yes, but those houses are so pretty, and the views are spectacular. I wonder how much they sell for now."

"Probably more than they did when you were a kid. Why? Are you thinking of buying one?"

"No. Although, I have been saving money to buy a house. I just haven't found anything that I love. Nothing is quite right. My mother says that's because I still want a house at the beach; she's not completely wrong."

"So why don't you live at the beach?"

"There is no ocean beach in Austin, and lakes don't quite do it for me."

"You could always come back to King Harbor."

"I have a life in Austin now. King Harbor is my past."

"Right now, it's your present," he said with a smile.

"For the next two weeks, but then I go back to reality."

"Well, since reality is still days away and we're now in open water, why don't we let this baby run?"

"Sounds good," she said. "Show me what you've got."

"Right back at you," he said.

She laughed. "It's your boat. You're in charge."

"Words I never thought I'd hear you say."

"Don't get used to it."

For the next thirty minutes, they worked together in easy accord. Devlin was quick, agile, and calmly efficient. He gave orders with a smile that sent tingles down her spine. And as they worked the sails and rode the waves, she felt incredibly happy. With the sun on her head and the wind at her back, she felt transported back in time to days spent out on the ocean with her dad. On the water, everything had seemed possible, and problems had floated far away. She'd missed this feeling of freedom, of being untethered, of flying across the sea.

And when she looked at Devlin, she saw the same pure joy in his eyes. Muscles rippling, his body powering the sails, he was completely in his element. He'd been born for this, and he'd found a way to combine passion and business.

She almost felt bad about wanting to beat him—almost. Because as much as he loved this boat, she had a feeling her father loved it just as much.

He turned his head and met her gaze. "What?" he asked.

"You look like a kid in a candy shop."

"The sea is my candy shop. I love it out here. I think you love it, too."

"I do," she admitted.

"What do you think about the *Wind Warrior*?"

"She might be the best boat my father ever built."

He grinned. "Probably. Getting worried about your chances?"

"I'm sure you'd like that, but no."

"You're good, too, Hannah. I should have expected that. Your father was your teacher."

"Yes, he was. My happiest childhood memories are of us sailing together."

"Did your mother like to sail?"

"Not at all. And the more she resented my dad's devotion to boat building, the more she grew to dislike boats. I don't think she's been out on the water in years."

"Did she marry again?"

"She did—four years ago. Her husband is a contractor,

and he's a good man. He treats her well." She paused. "Have you heard any more from your mother?"

"No. I was thinking about texting her, but maybe I should give her some space."

"Maybe. It has only been a day."

"True. Do you want to take the wheel?"

"You're giving up control?"

"I can give up control, especially when there's a beautiful woman involved."

She laughed. "That's a good line. How many times have you said that?"

"I can't remember ever saying it."

"Sure," she said, moving in behind the wheel. She'd thought Devlin would take a step back, but he remained right behind her, so close she could feel the heat of his body. "You must not trust me if you have to hover." She turned her head, feeling the warmth of his breath on her cheek.

"It's not that I don't trust you," he murmured.

"Then what is it?"

"I like being close to you."

She shivered at his words. "You're a big flirt, Devlin." Distracted, the boat shifted, and she stumbled.

He slid his hands onto her waist to steady her, but then he left them there. If she leaned back, she'd be right up against his very muscular chest. She blew out a breath. "Maybe you should take over again."

"You're doing fine. You're just distracted."

"Because you're distracting me," she retorted.

"If you really want me to move away, I will. Or…" He reached past her and put the boat on autopilot. "We could see where this attraction could go…"

He turned her around, and she felt incredibly torn.

Then Devlin moved forward, putting his hands back on her waist, his gaze questioning as he leaned in, and for the life of her she could not find the will to say no.

And when his lips touched hers, the voice in her head started yelling *yes, yes, yes*.

Closing her eyes, she gave in to the desire sweeping through her, opening her mouth to his, taking the kiss where she wanted it to go. She wrapped her arms around his neck, pressing her breasts against his solid chest, slipping her leg between his.

The chemistry between them was incredible, the hunger running through her strong and irresistible. She thought she could keep on kissing him forever…

If only her brain wasn't trying to leap into action, wasn't trying to remind her that Devlin was the enemy.

But he didn't feel like an enemy, and she was having trouble remembering why she didn't like him.

And then a loud thud from below broke them apart.

"What was that?" she asked in alarm.

"I have no idea, but I'm going to find out. Stay here."

CHAPTER SIX

HANNAH STEADIED her hand on the wheel as Devlin moved across the deck and down the stairs, not sure if she should be grateful or unhappy that their impulsive kiss had come to an end.

Relieved, she told herself. *You should be relieved.*

She frowned, hearing Devlin talking... *What the hell?* She'd thought it was just the two of them on the boat.

Since Devlin wasn't shouting with alarm, she ignored his order to stay put, and went down the stairs, into the salon and galley kitchen that separated two staterooms. Standing in the doorway of one of those staterooms was a boy of about ten or eleven. He had blond hair and big brown eyes and was wearing shorts, a T-shirt, and tennis shoes.

"Who's this?" she asked.

"This is Mason Rogers," Devlin said. "He apparently got on the boat when I wasn't looking."

"Hi, Mason. I'm Hannah."

"Don't be nice to him," Devlin said. "He's a stowaway. We should make him walk the plank."

Mason's eyes widened. "You're going to throw me in the water?"

"I should," Devlin said.

Despite his firm tone, Mason didn't look too worried by Devlin's threat. Clearly, the two of them knew each other.

"Where does your mom think you are?" Devlin asked Mason.

"At baseball practice, but I don't like baseball. I'm terrible at it. I want to be a sailor like my dad."

Hannah smiled at the fervor in his eyes. Mason definitely had the bug. She could see the understanding lurking in Devlin's eyes as well. He'd probably been a lot like Mason as a kid.

"Are you going to tell my mom?" Mason asked.

"You're going to tell her. Right now." Devlin pulled out his phone.

"Can't we sail for a little longer?" Mason pleaded. "She won't let me out of the house for a month after this."

"We'll finish our sail, but you're still going to call her now, so she doesn't worry about you." He pushed a button on his phone, then handed it to Mason. "It's ringing."

Mason let out a sad sigh, and then said, "Mom, it's me. I'm not at baseball practice. I'm sailing with Devlin." He paused. "Mr. Blackthorne, I mean. He's going to bring me back after we're done sailing." He listened for another minute, then handed Devlin the phone. "She wants to talk to you."

"Hi, Erica," Devlin said. "Mason is fine. He snuck on board when I wasn't looking. Don't worry. It will be fine. It's not an inconvenience. I'll bring him home in an hour or so. Does that work? Great." He ended the call and put the phone into his pocket. "I should make you spend the rest of the sail in the closet you were hiding in," he told Mason.

Mason gave him a pleading look. "Can I please come up on the deck? It's hot down here. I'll do whatever you say."

"You will definitely do whatever I say," Devlin told him. "And you'll put on a life jacket, too."

"Okay," Mason said eagerly.

He gave her a smile as they followed Mason up the stairs.

"Looks like we got ourselves a chaperone," he said. "Disappointed?"

"Not at all. It's probably a good thing. We don't even like each other," she said, trying to ignore the shiver running down her spine.

He laughed. "Don't we, Hannah?"

Okay, so she did like him, probably more than she should. And watching Devlin answer Mason's endless questions while also allowing him to help sail the boat was touching and heartwarming. Devlin was patient and kind. "You might be a Blackthorne," she told him, "but you are nothing like your father."

"I'll take that as a compliment." He moved to the side as Mason hung on to the wheel. The boat was back on autopilot, but Mason probably still felt like he was in charge, and she'd never seen a happier kid.

"I'm going to be a sailor when I grow up," Mason declared, glancing back at them. "I'm already saving my allowance, so I can get a boat. I want to race this summer, but my mom says it's expensive and we can't afford it."

Devlin frowned. "I'm sure she appreciates you saving your allowance."

"Do you think I could help you and make more money?" Mason asked.

"We'll see."

As Mason looked back out at the water, Devlin said quietly, "Mason's dad died last year."

"I'm sorry to hear that," she murmured.

"Mason's mom, Erica, is our admin at the Boatworks. She has been struggling on her own trying to take care of Mason and his two younger sisters. I've tried to help, but I need to do better by them. I know how much Mason loves boats. I should have anticipated that he'd try to stow away. I caught him hiding in the boat when it was still in the shop."

"He's got the fever."

Devlin grinned back at her. "We both know the feeling, don't we?"

"I'd almost forgotten, but it's coming back to me."

"Good. Because you should never forget this."

She knew he was talking about sailing, but she thought there were a lot of things about this day that she wasn't going to be able to forget, no matter how hard she tried.

"I'm sorry we were interrupted," he said softly. "Things were just getting interesting."

"I didn't come here to give you *interesting*."

"It was an unexpected side benefit."

She shook her head in confusion. "I don't get you, Devlin. I yelled at you. I told you I was going to beat you in your favorite race, and you want to kiss me? What's that all about?"

"Hell if I know," he said with a laugh. "What can I say but that I find you incredibly attractive? I also like the way you're fighting for your father. I respect fierce loyalty. As for the race, I also love a good competitor."

"Even if you lose?"

"I don't intend to lose."

"I'm sure you don't. You're a man who probably wins a lot."

"Because I work hard." An irritated gleam entered his eyes. "I'm sure you don't believe that, but it's true."

"You work hard, but you also work in your family's company. You didn't have to scrape your way to the top."

"True, but don't you work for your mother?"

She frowned at the reminder. "That's different. We're not rich."

"But your mother's company is successful, so you didn't have to start in the real estate business at the bottom."

"Fine, point taken. I had a leg up, and so did you."

"But what we've done after that is all on us. And, frankly, my father is creating more problems for me right now than he's solving."

"My mom has done that, too. She got in the middle of one of my deals and almost lost it for me. But she thought she knew best. I wanted to kill her."

"I know the feeling."

"Devlin, look—dolphins." Mason pointed to two dolphins frolicking in the water.

"Cool," Devlin said. "But you have to pay attention to what you're doing, Mason. You need to be ready and let me know if the wind changes direction."

"I will," Mason promised.

Devlin stepped over to the wheel to give Mason more instructions.

The wind had changed direction, she thought.

She just didn't know if she should keep sailing into it.

They got back to the harbor a little after three and headed toward the parking lot behind the Yacht Club. "Do you have your car?" Devlin asked.

"No. I walked here."

"I'll give you a ride."

"You need to take Mason home."

"That will only take a few minutes and your house is less than a mile from the Boatworks, so it's not out of my way. Why don't you come with me?"

She really needed to start saying no to Devlin's invitations, but maybe not just yet. "All right." She slid into the front seat of Devlin's black Audi, not surprised he'd have an expensive and sophisticated car. For all Devlin's casual, back-to-nature style, he was still a Blackthorne.

Mason talked all the way to his house, jumping from one question to the next, without waiting for an answer. But as soon as they pulled up in front of his house, he fell silent.

A woman stepped out of the modest one-story structure. She wore jeans and a knit top that revealed her thin frame. Her brown hair was pulled back in a ponytail and even from a distance, Hannah thought she looked tired. The door behind her opened and two little girls came onto the porch. They looked to be twins, probably about three years old.

"Do you want to meet my mom?" Mason asked her, a hopeful gleam in his eyes.

He probably thought introducing her to his mother would be a good distraction and put off his punishment that much longer.

"I think I'll stay here."

"Come, say hello," Devlin urged. "Erica is a big fan of your father's. She was furious when he was let go. I'm sure she'd like to meet you."

Well, when he put it like that, she could hardly say no. She got out of the car and followed Devlin and Mason across the overgrown lawn.

"I'm so sorry, Devlin," Erica said immediately. "I'm really embarrassed that Mason snuck away from baseball practice and got onto your boat. And you, young man, are in big trouble," she told her son. "Go in the house and take your sisters with you. We'll talk about your punishment in a minute. Oh, and say thank you to Mr. Blackthorne before you go."

"Thank you, Dev—Mr. Blackthorne," Mason said, then ran up the steps and grabbed the hands of his two little sisters, taking them into the house.

"I hope Mason didn't interrupt your date." Erica gave her a speculative look.

"We're not on a date," she said quickly.

"This is Hannah Reid," Devlin said, smiling at her hasty comment. "Frank's daughter. And, as she said, we were not on a date. I was just showing her the boat."

"Oh, Hannah," Erica said, her smile filling with warmth. "I can't believe I'm finally meeting you. Frank talks about you all the time. But he said you rarely get out to Maine anymore."

"It has been a few years."

"I'm Erica Rogers. Devlin probably told you that. I'm the admin at the Boatworks. I work closely with your father." Her lips tightened as she gave Devlin a hard look. "Or at least I did until this nonsense happened."

Devlin put up a hand. "You know it wasn't my doing."

"It's still wrong. How is Frank feeling, Hannah? I've called and texted, but he doesn't reply."

"He's all right. He hasn't felt like talking to anyone, but he is considering his options."

"And I'm still working on getting Frank his job back, Erica," Devlin put in. "It's not a done deal as far as I'm concerned."

"I hope not," Erica said. "Losing Frank would cripple the company. In fact, as soon as the rumors start taking hold, we're going to be dealing with lots of questions."

"I'm aware of that. Putting that situation aside," Devlin said. "Mason told me that he'd like to participate in the kids' sailing program this summer, but he needs a boat."

Erica frowned. "He should not have bothered you with that."

"Maybe I can help."

"You've done more than enough for us, Devlin. You are not going to buy Mason a boat. He's eleven. He can wait. And after what he did today, I should not be rewarding his behavior."

"He loves being on the water," Devlin said. "Like Jim."

She gave him a sad smile. "He is his father's son."

"If we can't find him a boat, we can make him one. It's what we do."

"A seven-foot dinghy isn't on our luxury boating product list," she said with a dry smile.

"I have an idea," Devlin said. "We'll talk on Monday."

"All right. It was nice to meet you, Hannah. Will you tell Frank I'm thinking about him?"

"I will."

As Erica went into the house, they returned to the car.

"How did her husband die?" she asked, as she fastened her seat belt.

"Car accident. One minute he was there, and the next he was gone. Although, to be honest, I think most deaths feel like that, even when you have warning. There's never enough time."

His voice grew rough, and she remembered a night from a long time ago when her father had brought home a drunken, angry, heartbroken Devlin. She'd been sixteen and had just arrived for the summer. Devlin had been twenty-one and a recent college graduate.

Her father had told her to go back into her room, but she'd heard a little of what they'd said to each other, and she knew that a girl Devlin had been dating had passed away. She'd never really heard the details. Her father wouldn't talk about it, and she hadn't seen Devlin again after that summer. She'd heard he'd gone traveling, taking time off to figure out his next move. But she'd wondered if he hadn't gone somewhere to heal.

Glancing over at him now, she saw his hard profile, and wondered if he was remembering, too.

"Was that how it felt to you?" she asked.

He gave her a sharp look. "What are you talking about?"

"I know you suffered a loss, Devlin. I was at the house the night my father let you sleep on our couch a long time ago."

"You were there? I don't remember seeing you."

"I was in my room when he brought you back from the bar. You were wasted and sad."

"Were you eavesdropping?"

"Yes, but I only heard bits and pieces, and my dad refused to fill in the blanks. He told me not to tell anyone you had been there." She paused, waiting for him to say something, but he remained silent. "What happened, Devlin?"

"It was a long time ago, Hannah."

"Someone you cared about died. Was it sudden? Was it an accident?"

He didn't answer, but he did make a turn. He drove down a street that dead-ended at the beach, then turned off the engine, staring out at the sea once more.

"Are you going to tell me?" she asked tentatively.

His gaze swung to hers. "I don't know. I might regret it."

"Then maybe you shouldn't. It's personal, and I'm being too pushy—as usual."

He blew out a breath. "She wasn't anything like you, Hannah."

She didn't know if she should take that as an insult or a compliment. Maybe this conversation was a bad idea... But it was too late now.

CHAPTER SEVEN

"AMY WAS QUIET," Devlin said. "She was a people pleaser and a peacemaker and probably one of the sweetest people I've ever known. We met at the beginning of our senior year at Yale. She was a photographer and was taking photos of one of my sailing races for the college newspaper. We started talking, and we never stopped."

She could hear the love in his voice and felt an odd tingle of envy run through her, but she could not be jealous of this poor young woman who had died too young. "What happened to her, Devlin?"

"She was diagnosed with a rare form of bone cancer right after Christmas. We'd only been dating since October, and it seemed surreal. She thought she'd pulled a muscle in yoga, but when the pain didn't go away after a few weeks, she finally went to the doctor. It was a devastating diagnosis. We were twenty-one years old. It seemed impossible that she could suddenly be that sick when she was fine before that."

"I can't even imagine."

"The disease moved very quickly. Her parents wanted to take her home, but she was too sick to move, so they got a rental by the school and took care of her there until she went into the hospital. I spent a lot of time with them. We were all trying to be positive, but by the end of March, she was gone."

"That is so fast."

He stared out at the sea. "I don't know how I made it through the last quarter of school. I was completely numb. But I felt compelled to graduate, because Amy had made me promise that I would, that I'd walk across the stage for both of us. That's what I did."

There was so much pain in his voice, her heart broke for him. "I'm sorry, Devlin. Maybe you should stop talking."

He ignored her suggestion, turning his gaze on her. "Even though I knew her death was coming, it still shocked the hell out of me. I wasn't ready. I don't think she was, either. We had only ever talked about her getting better, about the future she'd have—*we'd* have. When I would leave her at night, I'd tell her I'd see her soon. And she'd smile and say she couldn't wait. But one night she slipped away while I was sleeping. Her dad came and woke me up, but it was over. I never got to say good-bye."

"That's awful."

"Worst experience of my life."

"Was anyone there for you, Devlin?"

"My parents came down once, but they didn't know Amy; they had never met her. It felt awkward, and I just wanted to be with Amy, so I asked them to go home—same with my brothers and cousins. I knew they wanted to help, but I felt like Amy and her parents and I were in this narrow tunnel, and there wasn't room for anyone else."

"That sounds kind of lonely, but I guess I understand."

"Maybe it would have been different if they'd known her, but they'd never met her when she was healthy and after she got sick, she didn't want to see anyone."

She nodded, still hating the fact that Devlin had gone through such a tragedy on his own.

"After I graduated," he continued, "I came here to King

Harbor. I worked at the Boatworks, thinking I could find some peace in this place that I loved so much, but after the grief left, I was filled with anger. I drank a lot—way too much. One night, I got into a fight. The bartender called your dad. Frank came and pulled me out of the bar and took me to your house. He knew I couldn't handle dealing with my parents at that moment."

"That's what he told me when he went to get you, that you were going through a tough time and that you had enough to deal with."

"That night was a turning point for me. I knew I had to get my shit together, but I had to do it somewhere else. I got a job crewing on a luxury yacht, and I spent the next two years traveling the world."

"Where did you go?"

"Everywhere—Iceland, Norway, Europe, Spain, Morocco, Tahiti…the list goes on. Eventually, I started feeling better, happier."

"The ocean did its job."

"Yes," he agreed, giving her a smile. "It healed me."

"I'm surprised you ever came back."

"I found myself missing King Harbor. I wanted to accomplish more with my life. My dad told me I could take over the Boatworks if I was willing to work my way up, so I took a job there. Eventually, the manager decided to leave, and I took over."

"Did you ever consider that my father should have taken over?" she couldn't help asking.

"I didn't have to consider it; my dad offered Frank the job before he gave it to me."

"I never heard that," she said doubtfully.

"Your father turned it down, Hannah. He said he didn't want to manage a company or employees or have to worry about profit and loss; he just wanted to design and build boats."

"That does sound like him. My mom wanted him to move up the work ladder, but he always said he liked what he was doing. She couldn't understand his lack of ambition, because when she does something, she wants to be the best and to be in charge."

"There's nothing wrong with that; I'm much the same way."

"My dad is different. He wants to do the best work he can, but he doesn't care about being in charge."

"What about you? Who do you take after, Hannah?"

"I'm probably a bit of both of them. I'm ambitious and I want to be successful at what I do. But I also want more than work in my life. I can't believe I've been too busy to come back to King Harbor for five years. That's wrong. I need to find a better balance. I'm actually thinking the next two weeks will be a good time for me to reassess my goals. Plus, I get to catch up with my dad, maybe some old friends, and, of course, beating you will be the icing on the cake."

"Ouch."

She smiled. "I know it won't be easy. You're very good."

"You're not bad, either. I wouldn't mind having you on my boat. I still need a second crew member."

"I have no doubt you can find someone exceptional. And this race with my dad will help bridge the distance that's grown between us. Plus, it gives my dad something else to think about, and he needs that right now."

"I know."

"Thanks for telling me your story, Devlin. It's not one that many people seem to know, even in this small town where gossip is a favorite hobby."

"I've never felt compelled to share it. I'm sure people have talked about it behind my back, but it was a long time ago— ten years. Sometimes, I can't believe it has been that long. Anyway, now you know the story of why your father had to rescue me that night."

She gave him a thoughtful gaze. "Why did you tell me?"

"You already knew some of it. And I didn't think you were going to drop it."

"Both of those things are true, but I don't believe either one is the real reason."

He shifted in his seat, giving her a direct look. "Maybe I wanted you to know another side of me, Hannah."

"A side you don't show many people."

"No, I don't." He paused. "Amy was in my life for less than a year, but she had an impact on me. Her death made me realize that I didn't want to waste a second of my life going down a path that wasn't right for me. When I was in college, I was a business major. I sailed on the side, of course, but I was going down the path of becoming an executive for Blackthorne Enterprises. After Amy died, once I went off on my own, and started really living my life, I realized that wasn't what I wanted at all. Maybe you think it was a cop-out to go to the Boatworks, since it was also a Blackthorne company—"

"I don't," she interrupted. "It was exactly what you wanted to do. Why wouldn't you work there?"

"Right? It was part of the family business, but it felt like I was the only person who had the desire or the ability to take it over. Anyway, you asked me why I told you my story, and it's this: I may be a Blackthorne, Hannah, but I'm also me. I'm my own man. I'd prefer to be judged by what I do and not by what my family does."

"That's fair. I do recognize that you're an individual, Devlin."

"Good. Because when I kiss you again, I want you to know who you're kissing."

A shiver ran through her, not only at his words, but also the look in his eyes. "I didn't say you could kiss me again."

And suddenly the Devlin grin was back. "You didn't say I couldn't. Last chance."

He might have foreshadowed his intent, but there wasn't enough time to say no or to pull away… At least, that's what she told herself when he kissed her, and she kissed him back.

These kisses were different from the ones they'd exchanged on the boat. They were filled with emotion, with a feeling of connectedness, with a desire to bring Devlin out of the pain he'd just gotten lost in. And when they broke apart, she felt more than a little shaken by the depth of her desire. She wanted this man, and she didn't know what to do about it. Their relationship was so complicated. Part of her still wanted to hate him on her father's behalf, but the bigger part of her wanted to explore the unbelievable chemistry between them.

"Hannah?" he questioned.

"You should take me home." When he made no move to start the car, she added, "Maybe now."

"What are you afraid of?"

"Right now—myself," she said candidly.

"I'm glad you didn't say you were afraid of me."

"I don't like how you make me feel, Devlin."

"How do I make you feel?"

"Wild, reckless, impulsive…"

"And those are bad things?" he said, a sexy smile curving his lips.

"I was in a year-long relationship until six months ago."

"That's right, the three-day engagement. What happened with that?"

"He panicked. After I said yes, he started wondering if he was doing the right thing. He decided to talk to his ex-girl-friend one last time."

"That's not good."

"No, it wasn't. He went back to her. He said he was doing me a favor; that I should find someone who could put me first. That's what I deserved."

"It is what you deserve."

"But not so easy to find. Anyway, I'm not really looking

to get involved with anyone. I want to be on my own for a while."

"I'm not looking for a relationship, either," he returned. "But we could have fun."

"We probably could. But from past experience, I can say that I don't like the part when the fun ends. I'm not ready to do it again. So, why don't you take me home?"

He slowly nodded. "All right." He started the engine, and they drove to her dad's house in silence.

She didn't know what to say. Devlin seemed to have run out of words as well.

"Doesn't look like Frank is home," he finally said, turning in to her empty driveway.

"He'll be back soon."

"After he finishes trying to work a miracle on Howard Palmer's boat?"

She smiled. "I never said it was Mr. Palmer's boat."

"We both know it is."

"Well, it doesn't matter. And just in case you're thinking that I now have a soft spot for you and I won't want to beat you in the race, you need to know you're wrong. Because I am going for that trophy."

He grinned back at her. "I wouldn't expect anything less. But that trophy is coming home with me. I'll see you soon, Hannah."

"Good-bye, Devlin." She got out of the car and hurried into the house, wishing she didn't already miss him.

───────

Devlin drove the few blocks between Frank's house and the Boatworks with emotions that were all over the map. He didn't regret telling Hannah about Amy. Although, he questioned why he'd felt the need to share with her a story he had never discussed with anyone outside of his family. But somehow, the words had just spilled out of him.

It had felt surprisingly good. He felt freer, which was strange, because it had been ten years since Amy died, and he'd thought he'd put it all aside a long time ago. Apparently, he had not let go of it completely, maybe because he had never expressed the loneliness he'd felt while going through the experience on his own.

He didn't blame anyone in his family, though. He'd pushed them away. Carrying the burden alone had somehow made him feel more noble, more in love with a girl he'd known less than a year.

Would they have lasted if she hadn't died?

He had no idea.

Had Amy been the great love story of his life? Or was their story only the most tragic?

He'd never been able to answer those questions.

Parking in the lot in front of the Boatworks, he forced thoughts of the past out of his head. When he entered the building, instead of going upstairs to his apartment, he moved down the stairs leading into the basement. The large room spanned the entire building and was a crowded but organized storage center. He walked past filing cabinets holding business information and tax returns going back years, old furniture discarded when the upstairs offices had been redone, and boxes and boxes of boat parts, tools, and other miscellaneous supplies.

In the back of the room was exactly what he was looking for—a seven-foot fiberglass boat known as the *Optimist*, the most popular single-handed sailing dinghy for kids under the age of fifteen. He'd sailed this boat in his very first race nineteen years ago. He'd come in third, and he'd been mad as hell. He'd wanted to win so badly. He'd wanted to prove to his father that he was good as he was, because his father had won his first race at age ten.

"Devlin?"

He started at the sound of his father's voice, wondering if he'd somehow conjured him up with his thoughts.

"Devlin?" his father called out once more. "Where are you?"

"Basement," he yelled, moving around a filing cabinet as his dad came down the stairs.

His father wore black pants and a dark-blue shirt open at the collar, his pepper-gray hair styled, an air of expensive cologne about him. He certainly looked better than he had earlier in the day.

"Dad, what are you doing here? I thought you went back to Boston."

"I changed my mind. What are you doing?"

"Checking to see if my old boat was still here." He waved his hand toward the *Optimist*. "And she is."

"Why do you care about that old boat?"

"There's a kid who needs a boat for the summer sailing program. It's Mason, Erica Rogers's son. I don't know if you remember her…"

"I know who Erica is. I was sorry to hear about her husband."

"It's a sad situation, and I'd like to make it better. Mason loves to sail. I was wondering if this old boat has some more races in her."

"I'm sure she does. Maybe even a win."

"It took me three years to get a win in this boat. I kept losing to Kyle Hartman. It made me crazy."

"I remember," his dad said with a faint smile. "Your mother told me I should stop putting so much pressure on you to win. But I wanted you to know what victory felt like. And eventually you did."

There was a familiar note of pride in his father's voice now. While he was happy he'd done something that his father was proud of, he couldn't help but think that Blackthorne pride also caused a hell of a lot of problems.

"Now you win every year," his dad added.

"Well, the last few years I've had a fantastic partner."

His father's expression went cold. "I didn't come here to talk about Frank."

"But we still need to talk about him. You're letting a personal issue get in the way of business, and that's not like you."

His father stiffened. "Frank had no right to talk to Claire and get in the middle of my marriage."

"Maybe Mom put him in the middle."

"He went there willingly, but, as I said, I didn't come to talk about Frank. I wanted to let you know that your mother is fine. She's in Paris."

"Paris?" he echoed. "She went to France?"

"That's where Paris is," Graham said tightly.

"Have you spoken to her? Is she coming home? Are you going after her?"

"I have not talked to her. But I've been informed that she's fine and she has a place to stay, so you don't need to worry about her."

"I was more worried about your marriage than her safety. Why don't you talk to her? She's clearly upset."

"Your mother embarrassed me. She ranted in front of our friends and business associates about nonsense. I have never done anything but love and respect and provide for her. She needs to get over this birthday depression madness and come home and apologize."

"You don't have anything to apologize for?" he dared to ask.

"My relationship with your mother is not your business, Devlin."

"She made it everyone's business the other night."

"That was unfortunate. But this will be over soon. Your mother will be back."

He hoped his father's confidence was not misplaced.

"Anyway, I'll be going to Boston in the morning," Graham continued. "I'd appreciate it if you'd check in on your grandmother while I'm gone. Pam and Joe will certainly do their part, but without Claire here, I worry about her."

"I'd be happy to check in on her. When are you coming back?"

"I'm not sure—a few days."

Which meant he'd have to wait a few more days to resolve the situation with Frank. That wasn't going to make Hannah happy.

"I should get going," his dad said.

"Wait." He gave in to an impulse he would probably regret. "Do you ever miss sailing, Dad?"

"I sail," his father said with a frown.

"You cruise on luxury yachts. You don't work the sails. You don't ride the wind, not the way you used to. I need a partner for the race. No one else in the family is available. What about you?"

"I haven't raced in years."

"Not since Uncle Mark died," he acknowledged. "I know it wouldn't be the same, but it could be fun. And you might have the added bonus of beating Frank."

His father's gaze sharpened. "What are you talking about?"

"Frank is going to race another boat with his daughter, Hannah. He's determined to beat me, to show he's the reason we've won the race the last several years."

"He won't be able to find another boat as good as ours."

"No, but he's a damned good racer, one of the best there is. His daughter is good, too. I need a partner who has experience, likes to compete, and refuses to lose. Sound like anyone you know?"

A gleam entered his father's eyes. "Are you trying to handle me, Devlin?"

"That depends. Is it working?"

His father gave him a long stare. "We can't let Frank win that race."

"I can't do it alone. If you want the *Wind Warrior* to come in first and double its value, then you either need to race, or I need to get Frank back in the company and back on the boat."

"I'll...think about it," Graham said. "But don't give me ultimatums, Devlin. You may run the company, but I own it."

"I can't run the company with my hands tied behind my back," he said tersely. "You need to respect me and my ability to make the Boatworks profitable. You might want to think about that, too."

His father turned and left the room without further comment. He blew out a breath, not sure where they'd ended up but glad he'd put his cards on the table. His father wasn't the only one with Blackthorne pride. He'd made the Boatworks more profitable than it had ever been, and it was about time his father recognized that fact.

CHAPTER EIGHT

HANNAH MANAGED to avoid Devlin for three whole days. In fact, she'd just started to relax when she ran into him on the sidewalk in front of the Yacht Club on Wednesday night. He wore tan slacks and a white button-down shirt. His hair was damp, his cheeks cleanly shaven, and there was a sparkle in his brown eyes.

As their gazes met, her stomach did a happy little somersault, making a mockery of her resolve to forget about him.

"This is a nice surprise," he said. "I didn't know you were coming to Jessica's party."

"Her mom invited me when I signed up for the race on Sunday. Jessica and I were friends in elementary school. I didn't realize you and Jessica were now friends."

"Jessica works at the distillery."

"Right. She's another Blackthorne employee; I forgot."

He smiled as she rolled her eyes. "Our employees are not indentured servants. We pay quite well," he teased. "But I'm actually better friends with Vince, her fiancé. He runs the fish and chips café on the wharf—The Flying Fish."

"That's a new one for me."

"He opened about two years ago and does a good business. You should try it some time." He paused. "How's the *Daisy Mae* coming along? Have you taken her out yet?"

"We're going to do that tomorrow. My dad has been whipping her into shape. What about you? Have you found a racing partner?"

"Possibly. I'm still waiting to get a firm commitment from my dad."

"Your dad?" she echoed in surprise. "I thought you said he never raced, not since his brother died."

"Well, we had an interesting chat on Sunday night, and when he heard you and Frank were going to be competing against us, he told me he might be willing to do it. Apparently, beating your father has provided much-needed incentive."

"My dad is also fired up at the prospect of taking your family down. Not that he's angry with you," she said hastily. "He's told me several times that he understands you're caught in the middle."

"I'm glad to hear that. Your father has been a good friend, a mentor to me. I hate that I'm letting him down. But I still think with a little time we can work it all out."

"By the time you work it out, my father may decide to move on. He's been getting calls from other companies."

"Well, I hope he'll talk to me before he makes a decision. Maybe you could pass that on to him."

"Sure. Has there been any word from your mother?"

"I know she's in Paris, but that's all I know."

"Springtime in Paris doesn't sound bad."

"I'm hoping it's just a vacation and not a permanent change of address. But I'm going to have to wait and see how that plays out as well. Shall we go inside?"

"Sure." She was actually a little relieved to have Devlin by her side. She hadn't seen Jessica in years, and she had no idea who else would be at the party, if she'd have anyone to talk to or if she would just be extremely uncomfortable. She'd almost chickened out from attending, but the past few days helping her dad work on the boat had been a little boring. She'd forgotten how detailed he was, and how lost he could get in his craft, forgetting she was there half the time.

She'd told herself not to take it personally, but the quiet had been getting on her nerves, so she'd decided to come to the party. At least, now she would know one person, even if it was the one person she'd been trying to avoid.

The banquet room in the Yacht Club was packed with people. Jessica certainly had a lot of friends, and most of those friends were eager to give Devlin a hug or a handshake. She felt a little invisible in his shadow, but it gave her a chance to look around the room.

There were a dozen round tables in the middle of the room and two long buffet tables that were already laden with food, although no one was eating yet. A bar by the French doors leading onto the cocktail deck had a good-sized line going. A couple of servers were walking through the party, offering appetizers.

Outside, there were more tables and more people. It was a beautiful evening, unusually warm, with the temperature lingering in the low seventies even at six o'clock at night.

"Have you all met Hannah?" Devlin asked, taking her hand and pulling her into his bright light.

She smiled at the three young women, all around her age. Two of them didn't look very happy to see Devlin's hand in hers. She wanted to pull away, but that seemed like it would draw more attention.

"Hannah, this is Diana, Georgia, and Caroline," he said.

"Hello. I'm Hannah Reid. I went to school with Jessica." She didn't recognize Diana or Georgia, but Caroline looked very familiar. "Wait a second. You're Caroline Richards?"

"I wondered if you'd remember me."

"Of course I do, but your hair wasn't red when I knew you. It threw me for a second."

"No, it was a dull brown. I got bolder as I got older."
Caroline let out an infectious laugh. "That should be my
slogan. Bolder and older. Anyway, it's nice to see you again,
Hannah. It has been a long time."

"It has."

"Devlin, why don't you come out on the patio with us?"
Diana suggested. "It's much cooler there. And the bar on the
deck is not nearly as crowded."

"I wouldn't mind getting a drink," Devlin said, gazing
down at her. "What about you?"

"I'm fine for now."

"I'll be back soon," he promised.

As Diana and Georgia walked Devlin outside, Caroline
gave her a speculative smile. "Don't be jealous, Hannah.
They've been trying to get Devlin's attention for the last three
years, and he's just not interested."

"I'm not jealous," she said quickly. "I'm not with Devlin. I
ran into him outside. My father works for him. Or he used to,
anyway." She paused as a tall brunette joined them. "Jessica!
Happy birthday!"

"Oh, my God," Jessica said with delight and amazement.
"Hannah. My mother told me she invited you. I was going to
call and see if you were coming, but I didn't have your
number. I'm so glad you came."

She gave Jessica a hug, thinking how pretty she was now
with her dark hair and dark eyes.

"I see you've reconnected with Caroline," Jessica added.
"Whitney is supposed to come, too."

"I'd love to see her, too."

"So, what have you been up to?" Jessica asked. "I heard
you're living in Austin, Texas."

"Yes. That's where my mom and I moved after we left
here. She started a real estate firm, and I became an agent a
few years ago."

"I always thought you'd do something with your dad and

with boats. You were mad about sailing."

"There wasn't any ocean in Austin, and I got caught up in other things."

"But you're racing on Memorial Day, my mom said."

"I am. I hope I'm up to the challenge. Luckily, I have my dad to lead the way."

"I can't believe your father isn't racing with Devlin this year." Jessica took a quick glance around, then lowered her voice and said, "But I've heard that your father is no longer working at the Boatworks, so I guess it makes sense. Although, none of us understand what happened."

"It's a complicated situation."

"Well, I'm sure Devlin won't be thrilled to lose Frank for the race. They've been unbeatable," Jessica said.

"I'm not thrilled at all," Devlin interrupted, handing her a glass of wine. "I hope white is good. I remembered you had a chardonnay the other night."

"It's fine. Thanks." She couldn't help noticing the renewed curiosity in Caroline's eyes, and even Jessica looked taken aback by Devlin's comment.

"Are you two friends?" Jessica asked. "I was thinking if you both came to the party that there might be tension after what happened to Frank."

"There's definitely tension," Devlin said, giving her an intimate look.

She felt a wave of heat run through her, hoping she was the only one who saw the glint of reckless humor in his eyes. But Caroline's knowing smile put an end to that foolish thought.

"Oh, well…" Jessica looked a bit confused by his comment.

She quickly stepped in. "My father's relationship with Devlin and the Boatworks is not my business. It's between them," she said, thinking that she probably should have had that thought before she went into Devlin's office and ranted like a crazy person.

If she hadn't gone to see him, they might not have talked at all, might not have gone sailing, might not have kissed...

"But the race is between all of us," Devlin said. "I'm looking forward to competing against Hannah and her father. By the way, happy birthday, Jess."

"Thank you."

Their conversation was interrupted by Jessica's mother, Grace, who stepped up to a microphone and urged everyone to go to the buffet.

"Shall we get some food?" Jessica asked.

"I'm game," Caroline said.

"You two go ahead," she said, knowing that Jessica needed to be at the front of the line.

"We'll talk later, Hannah," Jessica promised. "If not tonight, because I know it's crazy here, maybe we can get together on Saturday. We could go to tea at the Bickmore."

"That would be great."

"What about you, Caroline?" Jessica asked. "Can you join us?"

"Absolutely."

"Then it's a date."

As Caroline and Jessica moved away, Devlin slid closer to her, jostling her shoulder with his. "Looks like you and your friends are going to pick up right where you left off."

"It's great to see them again, but I think you were giving them the wrong idea."

"About what?" he asked with an unrepentant grin, as he turned to face her.

"Us. Not that there is an *us*, but you kind of implied there was."

"I don't know what you're talking about."

"That *tension* comment wasn't loaded?"

"Well, we do have a lot of tension. And do you really care what anyone thinks?"

"Don't you care? You're the one who lives here, who will face questions from your friends."

"My friends don't ask me questions, at least not about women."

"So, what happened to your fan club?" she asked, changing the subject.

"If you're referring to Diana and Georgia, they disappeared when I told them I needed to take you your wine."

She sighed. "I'm sure they got the wrong idea, too."

"Who says it's the wrong idea?"

"Have you dated either one of them?"

"God, no."

"Why do you say it like that? They're attractive, the right age, obviously interested…"

"Diana is a huge gossip; I don't like that. And Georgia has a laugh that's like fingernails on a chalkboard."

She smiled at his grimace. "I'm sure it's not that bad."

"Trust me, it is."

"Well, if you don't date them, who do you date?"

"No one you know."

"Seriously, Devlin, is there someone in your life?"

He leaned in and whispered in her ear. "Do you think I would have kissed you the way I did if there was?"

She shivered at the warm caress of his breath. "I guess not, but I don't know."

"I don't kiss more than one woman at a time."

"Well, we're done with kissing, so you're free to move on."

He smiled. "I've missed you, Hannah."

"It's been three days since we last saw each other."

"Good to know you've been counting the days, too."

"I haven't," she denied, knowing that was a blatant lie.

Every time she'd gone into town, she'd found herself looking for him.

"Devlin, Hannah, time to eat," Mrs. Varney said, interrupting their conversation. "You'll want to get your plate before I let the kids hit the buffet."

"We're on it," Devlin said, putting his hand on the small of her back.

As they moved toward the buffet line, Devlin was waylaid by more friends, and she managed to slip away from him, filling her plate and taking it out on the patio. Caroline was sitting alone at a table.

She waved Hannah over. "Come, sit." She patted the empty chair next to her. "I was beginning to feel like a wallflower."

"I doubt you could ever be that," she said, as she sat down.

Caroline smiled. "I see you've lost your shadow."

"If you're referring to Devlin, I think I'm *his* shadow. He's like the brightest star in the galaxy."

"He is, but don't tell him that."

"Trust me, I won't. He definitely doesn't need more confidence."

"I haven't met a Blackthorne who isn't confident. But Devlin is a good guy. I don't know what went down with him and your father, but I'm sure there's more to the story, because Devlin doesn't just let people go."

"His father got in the mix."

"Well, that makes more sense. Graham Blackthorne is definitely capable of letting people go."

"So, what are you doing now, Caroline?" she asked, wanting to change the subject.

"I'm the program director at the Center Theater."

"That sounds fun."

"It's small time, but I love putting on shows, and working with actors. We have a children's summer workshop, too, that's very popular. Oh, and I'm also engaged. My ring is getting resized. That's why I'm not wearing it tonight."

"That's all great. No wonder you look so happy."

"I feel very lucky."

"Where is your fiancé? I'd like to meet him."

"That will have to be another night. He's a fireman, and he's working tonight. What about you? Any men besides Devlin?"

"There's no Devlin."

"I think you might be wrong," Caroline said with a pointed look.

She turned and saw Devlin approaching with a full plate of food.

"It's just dinner," she told Caroline.

"Maybe it doesn't have to be."

When Devlin slid into the seat next to her, she found herself wondering the same thing.

CHAPTER NINE

DEVLIN LIKED HANGING WITH HANNAH, even if she did not like hanging with him. Actually, he thought she liked it just fine; she simply didn't want to admit it, which was why she spent most of their meal grilling Caroline on her personal life and all the latest King Harbor news.

It had been awhile since a woman had given him the cold shoulder, and he had to admit it made him want to find a way to change her mind. He hadn't felt such a hunger for a woman in a long time—the kind of hunger that kept him up at night, that made him turn the shower from hot to cold, that suggested he give the logical part of his brain a long vacation and let his desire dictate his actions.

"Devlin?"

He suddenly realized Hannah was giving him an odd look. He hoped none of his thoughts had actually come out of his mouth. "Sorry, what?"

"Do you want cake? I'm going to get a piece."

"I'll share yours."

"Not a chance. I never share cake. Caroline, what about you?"

"I'm in pre-wedding diet mode," Caroline said. "No cake for me."

"Fair enough," Hannah said, as she headed into the banquet room.

He found himself watching the sway of her hips as she walked away in a short little dress that clung to her curves and showed off her beautiful legs.

"You are in trouble," Caroline said, an amused look in her eyes. "I don't think you want cake; I think you want Hannah."

He grinned back at her. "What if I do?"

"I'd say be careful. She's leaving in two weeks."

"I'm aware. I'm not thinking that far in the future."

"Spoken like a true man."

He shrugged and sat back in his seat as Hannah returned to the table with two servings of chocolate cake. She put one plate in front of him and then took her seat. "I'm so glad Jessica still loves chocolate," she said. "Do you want a bite, Caroline?"

"I thought you said you don't share?" he teased. "Or was that only with me?"

"I'm offering a bite, not half."

Caroline put up her hand. "Don't tempt me. I'm actually going to take off. It was nice to catch up, Hannah. I'll see you Saturday at the Bickmore, and Devlin, I'm sure I'll see you around."

After Caroline left, they ate their cake in relative silence, conversation from the other partygoers washing around them.

The night was coming to an end, but he wasn't quite ready to let Hannah go, and he had a feeling as soon as she finished her cake, she'd be heading home.

"So, I found Mason a boat," he said. "A single-handed dinghy about twenty-five years old. It was the boat my father taught me how to sail in, and it was the first boat I ever raced. I wasn't sure it was still seaworthy, but it appears that it is."

"That's great. Have you told Mason?"

"I have. He's very excited. His mom signed him up for the sailing program, and in exchange he's going to do a lot more around the house to help out."

"That's a win for both Mason and Erica. You did a good thing, Devlin."

He was glad she thought so. "Blackthornes aren't all black."

She tipped her head to his point.

"How's your father doing?" he asked.

"He has been working long hours on the boat, so we haven't talked a lot, but every now and then I catch a look of frustration and worry on his face. His whole life has been his job. He doesn't know what to do with himself, where to go, if he doesn't go to the Boatworks. Thank goodness he has the *Daisy Mae* to work on, and the idea of beating you and your father is keeping him going."

"I know it's rough, Hannah. I actually gave my dad an ultimatum a few days ago."

Her eyes widened. "What do you mean?"

"I told him that we need Frank back at work and on the boat, and he needs to respect how I run the Boatworks or I should move on."

"You threatened to quit? What was his response?"

"He told me not to give him ultimatums and stormed out of the room. Then he went back to Boston, but I think he'll eventually come to his senses."

"I'm losing faith in that."

"It has only been a few days. He'll be back soon, and we'll talk again."

"I appreciate you taking the stance that you did. Thank you for going to bat for my dad."

His gaze met hers. "I just did what was right. I'm sure you thought it took me too long, but I hoped it wouldn't have to come to an ultimatum."

"Would you really leave the company? It's your family

business. You've worked hard to build it up. Could you walk away?"

"I don't want to, but I could, and I would. Hopefully, it doesn't come to that." He paused. "Your father asked Erica to box up his office. Did you know that?"

"No, I didn't. That sounds like he's giving up."

"I told her to go slow, but while we were talking, she showed me some old photos she'd found in Frank's filing cabinet, pictures of Frank and your mother and my parents. They were actually pretty good friends at one time."

She gave him a confused look. "I remember them being friendly, but not to the point where they spent time together."

"But they did. There are lots of pictures of our parents together. You're even in one of the shots. You were a chubby baby."

She frowned. "Where were these pictures taken?"

"Around town. The point is that the relationship between our fathers goes back a long time. There's a feeling of betrayal on both sides, with my mother in the middle."

"I'd like to see the photos."

"Sure. Why don't you come back there with me now?"

"It's late."

"It's eight thirty. King Harbor may be a sleepy town, but we don't go to bed this early. Did you drive here?"

"I walked. It's only a mile or so."

"You really like walking, don't you?"

She smiled. "I take it that you drove."

"Well, to be fair, I did have to pick up Jessica's present on the way. Why don't I drive you to the Boatworks and then after you see the photos, I'll take you home?"

She hesitated. "Okay, but I'm just going to look at the pictures and then leave."

"What else would we do?" he said with a laugh.

After saying good-bye to Jessica, they made their way out of the Yacht Club and into Devlin's car. The drive to the Boatworks took less than five minutes, which didn't give Hannah much of a chance to have second thoughts about spending more time with Devlin. Indecision was still rolling around in her head when he unlocked the door and waved her into the building.

The large structure was dark and completely empty, giving it a bit of a spooky feel with the skeleton of a boat taking up room on the main work floor. Devlin flipped on some lights as they made their way up to her dad's office, which was on the second floor.

It felt even stranger to walk into the office and see some of her dad's things in boxes. It brought home a sense of finality that she'd been trying to avoid. Maybe her dad was done at the Boatworks. Or at least he thought he was done.

"You should tell my dad what you said to Graham," she told Devlin, as he moved around the desk. "It might reassure him. Unless you weren't serious about your ultimatum?"

"I'm serious. I can certainly speak to Frank, but I was hoping to wait until after I had a definitive answer. I do have to warn you that while I might fall on my sword for your father, it could just mean we're both out of a job."

"It's difficult to believe your dad would let you go."

"It's really not," he said dryly.

"Well, I guess we can wait and see what happens, since he'll be back in a day or two." She let out a sigh as she looked around the office. "I can't imagine my dad not being here, but it's starting to feel more real now."

"Why don't we take this box upstairs?"

"To your apartment?" she asked quickly, a nervous tingle running through her.

"Does that make you uncomfortable?"

"Well, I don't know."

"You can trust me, Hannah. I hope you know that."

She did know that. She just wasn't sure she could trust herself. But she wasn't going to tell him that. "I'm not worried. I would like to see where you live. I hope it doesn't feel as creepy as it does down here. It's such a big building. Isn't it weird to be here by yourself?"

"I've never thought that," he said with a laugh, grabbing the box. "And, to be honest, there are lots of people who work long hours, including your father. He's often down here when I finally call it a day."

"Well, he doesn't have anyone to come home to."

"No, he doesn't," Devlin said, an odd note in his voice. "Neither do I."

"But that's the way you like it, right?"

"I've always thought so. Let's get out of here." He led the way upstairs, punching in a code to unlock his door.

She was expecting the apartment to look as sparse and barren as Devlin's office downstairs, but she was pleasantly surprised. The large living space had floor-to-ceiling windows overlooking the water. An open kitchen displayed state-of-the-art appliances and the living area and dining room were furnished with a mix of white and gray furniture, offset by colorful rugs, throw pillows, as well as some very tasteful art on the walls, many of which were framed images of boat and ocean scenes.

Beyond the wall art, there wasn't much of a nautical theme to Devlin's home. But there was a sense of warmth and comfort that was at direct odds with the feeling she'd experienced earlier.

"This is a beautiful space," she told him, as he set the box on the dining room table. "Was it professionally decorated?"

"My mother and grandmother had a hand in picking out the furniture."

"I had a feeling. But it still feels like you. And that's nice."

"I like it. Hopefully, you've gotten past the creepy feeling," he teased.

"I have. I can barely remember what's downstairs."

"My mother was insistent that I feel like I'd left work when I came home. Of course, she would have preferred I live at the estate full-time, but barring that, she was determined to make me comfortable here."

"Why don't you live at the estate? It's huge. I know there's a housekeeper and a chef and plenty of people to take care of your every need."

"It's not my style. It's too big."

"Too big? You're living all by yourself in a huge building."

"But this space is just right. And I'm close to work."

"You don't want your own house?"

"Asks the real estate agent," he teased.

"Guilty. I do like putting people in their own homes. Not that this isn't lovely, but it's still an apartment in a boat manufacturing company. I think it's better for people to have a bit more distance between work life and home life. My father probably could have saved his marriage by simply moving to the next town. My mom wanted to feel like when he was home, he was really home."

"I can see that. It doesn't matter to me, because I'm on my own." He opened the box and pulled out a photograph. "This one is from a long time ago."

She took the photo from his hands, then sat down at the table as she studied it. There were four people sitting at a restaurant table, toasting some occasion with four glasses of champagne. Her parents looked incredibly young, as did Graham and Claire. "They had to be in their late twenties or thirties. Is this at the Bickmore?" she asked, referring to the stately manor at the edge of downtown that had once belonged to a silent film star and then had been turned into a luxury hotel. Its dining room was currently being run by a

Michelin-starred chef, and the wealthy summer tourists kept the restaurant booked months in advance.

"It looks like it. My parents loved going there for dinner."

"It was always too expensive for my family. I only went there once for breakfast, and that seemed like a real treat." She frowned. "I don't even remember my parents like this."

"I don't remember my parents like that, either. But this photo feels more familiar."

The next picture he handed her had been taken at the beach. The four friends were standing on the bluff overlooking the ocean, a dozen colorful sails behind them. "This must have been at the races. I do recall that sweater my mom is wearing."

"Here's one of you." He handed her another photo.

This picture had been taken at Harbor Park. Her mother and Claire were sitting at a picnic table with her and a little boy while Graham and her dad were tending to a nearby grill. She was probably three years old in the photo and the boy a year or two older.

"I'm pretty sure that's Ross," Devlin said.

"I wonder where you were."

"Who knows?" he said with a shrug. "Probably running around on the playground." He handed her another picture. "This is the last one. It's from six years ago. I can tell because that's when we launched the *Rebel King*. It was right after I came back from traveling around the world. And it was probably the last boat my father had much to do with. Once I started working, he took a big step back."

Her father and Graham were pictured standing in front of a large yacht, and the camera had caught them in a moment of pure, happy friendship. They were smiling at each other with what appeared to be a great deal of pride. "If only we could get them to remember the way they used to feel about each other. What if we show them these pictures?"

"I'm not sure a bunch of old photos will do the trick."

"They might be a start."

"Well, your father has had the photos for years. I got them from his office, so I don't think he needs reminding."

"Then maybe show them to your dad when he comes back."

"That's a thought." He paused. "Do you want some wine? We could sit on the deck. It's a nice night."

She gave him a thoughtful look. "What are we doing, Devlin?"

"I just want to have a drink with you. In fact, instead of wine, I think we should have some Blackthorne Gold."

"I'm betting you have a very good bottle."

"I do. What do you say?"

"You're a hard man to say no to."

"That sounds like a yes. I'll get the bottle and the glasses."

He was headed to the bar before she could tell him that wasn't exactly a yes.

She'd just have one drink and then leave.

CHAPTER TEN

HANNAH OPENED the doors to the deck and stepped outside. It was a beautiful night with a full moon and a starry sky. She drew in a breath of cool air, the pretty view filling her with happiness. She had missed living by the ocean. She'd told herself that city lights were just as amazing, but tonight's view made that a lie.

Devlin came up next to her and handed her a glass of whisky. "What should we toast to?"

"I have no idea," she said with a laugh. "Our dads?"

"I don't think they deserve a toast. How about to us? To not looking too far into the future."

She saw the gleam in his eyes. "That seems a little reckless."

"Only if you want it to be."

"Why don't we drink to friendship?"

"That sounds a little boring."

"Then let's just drink."

They clinked their glasses together, and then she took a sip. The whisky slid down her throat, warm, smooth, and sexy...kind of like Devlin.

She really should have stuck to wine, or better yet, gone home.

"What do you think?" he asked.

"It's very good. I can see why your family has made a fortune in whisky."

"Let's sit down." He led her to a comfortable couch and flipped on the fire pit in front of it.

As the flames lit up the dark shadows of the deck, she sat down and leaned back against the soft cushions. "This is nice. Better than I thought it would be."

Devlin sat next to her, not leaving much space between them, and she was quite sure that was deliberate.

He stretched out his arm along the back of the couch, not touching her, but making her yearn for the feel of his hand on her shoulder. She took another sip of whisky and searched for a distracting topic. "How come you didn't go into the whisky business?" she asked.

"It's not interesting to me. I like to drink it. I don't want to make it or sell it. Fortunately, I have brothers and cousins who do, so the family business is in good hands." His hand crept closer to her shoulder, and she had to fight the urge to settle back against it. "How do you like working with your mother?" he asked.

"I enjoy being part of her company. I'm proud of her and everything she accomplished. When we first left King Harbor, we were barely scraping by. But my mom got to work, and she changed all that. She found another side of herself—the aggressive, ambitious, persuasive, and successful side. She said she never realized she was that good at business until she had to be. Now she loves it." Taking another sip of her whisky, she added, "It's ironic that my mother has turned out to be as big of a workaholic as my dad. Although, she does try to put her second husband first. She learned something from the divorce."

"And what about you? Is real estate your dream job? Is it what you want to do with the rest of your life?"

"That's a big question. I thought we just toasted to not thinking too far down the road."

"Good point. I'll shorten the time frame. Is selling real estate what you want to do for the next year?"

She smiled back at him. "Yes, maybe…I don't know," she said, sinking back against the couch, which put his warm hand on her shoulder, and she felt surprisingly content. "Being back in King Harbor has gotten me thinking about how much I've missed living by the ocean, being on the water whenever I can, seeing a multitude of stars over my head instead of city lights. This view is unbeatable. I do like living in Austin and seeing my mom all the time, and it's very fulfilling to put people in their dream houses."

"But…"

She wasn't sure she could express the restlessness in her soul. "I just want more outside of my job. I'm not sure exactly what. I do know that one day I want to have my own place. Beyond that, the possibilities are endless."

"How about buying a cottage on a hill overlooking the sea?"

"That would be lovely," she said with a wistful sigh. "But my job isn't near any pretty cottages by the sea."

"Where do you live now?"

"I have a one-bedroom apartment in a high-rise building. It's nice, but it doesn't feel like a home. I've never really decorated. When Gary and I were dating, we spent most of the time at his place. We almost bought a house together. We had actually put in an offer the day after we got engaged. That might have been part of his panic, too. It was a busy week— engagement ring, possible house purchase—and then it all ended."

"I'm sorry, Hannah."

"It hurt, but I know now it wasn't right. And I'm glad he

called it off before we got married. I just wish I'd picked up on the signs earlier."

"What signs? He asked you to marry him. That shows commitment."

"I'm talking about signs that he wasn't over his ex. He used to talk to her on social media. He said they were friends, and I believed him. But he was also still in touch with her parents. And his parents also spent time with the ex. It was all a little too close. I knew it in my gut; I just didn't want to see it. I had this picture in my head of happily ever after, and I didn't want to ruin it. Love is blind." She sipped her whisky. "Live and learn, right?"

"Sometimes the lessons are painful," he said, gently kneading her shoulder. "You'll find the right person for you."

"I hope so." She turned her head, gazing into his eyes, and the connection between them intensified. "You scare me, Devlin," she whispered.

"Why?"

"Because I'm feeling things that I don't want to feel. And you're not the right person, either. You don't want a relationship. And I think there's a good chance you're still in love with Amy."

His gaze darkened. "I'm not in love with Amy, but she'll always be a part of my past."

"Your first love. I haven't had much luck with men getting over their first love."

"Well, I can't go back to mine," he said tersely. He shifted on the couch, pulling his arm away from her shoulders. "I'll give you a ride home."

She sat up straight, giving him a wary look. "You're kicking me out? I didn't realize the subject of Amy was off-limits."

"It's not."

"Then why the sudden turnaround?"

He got to his feet. "I have an early meeting tomorrow."

"First time you've mentioned that," she said, standing up. "I was just being honest, Devlin. I guess I forgot that honesty can kill the mood. Sorry about that."

"Why would you be sorry? You said you don't want anything to happen. Now, it won't."

She walked back into his apartment, set her glass on the counter and grabbed her bag before heading to the door.

Devlin walked her down the stairs and out of the building without saying a word. The silence accompanied them on the very short drive to her dad's house.

"Wait," he said, as she put her hand on the door. "I'm not in love with Amy."

"Okay," she said carefully, seeing the unusually hard lines around his mouth and eyes.

"But you were right, Hannah. I'm not looking for a relationship, and you are. You want that picture in your head: the man, the house, the dog…"

"I actually like cats."

"Over dogs? No way."

She felt the tension ease between them. "Cats are wonderful."

"They don't care about you. Any lap will do."

"Not true. I do want another relationship, Devlin. But I'm not in a hurry to get into one, not at all. It's been a rough year, and I am happy to be on my own. It gives me a chance to figure out what I really want, not just in a man, but in a job, in a place to live, in my other relationships."

"That's good."

"It is." She gave him a smile. "I like you, Devlin. I'm wildly attracted to you, but it's probably also good that you remembered your early meeting, before we did something we'd regret."

"I don't think we'd regret it. I'm attracted to you, too, but I don't want to hurt you, Hannah."

"I don't want to hurt you, either. I wouldn't want you to

fall in love with me and then have to say good-bye," she teased.

His grin came back. "I appreciate you watching out for my heart."

"That's what friends do. Good night." She got out of the car and hurried into the house before she changed her mind and told him to hell with the future or possible regrets; they had right now, and that was enough. *But would it be enough?* Probably not.

When she entered the living room, she saw her dad standing at the window. He turned to her with a worried expression in his gaze.

"What's wrong?" she asked.

"What were you doing with Devlin?"

"He gave me a ride home from the party." She didn't bother to mention the last hour hanging out in his apartment. "Why do you look upset?"

"I'm not upset; I'm worried. He's not for you."

She was surprised by his terse words. "I didn't say he was for me, but I thought you liked him."

"I do like him, but he goes through women like water. I think it has something to do with the woman he loved and lost. But that doesn't matter when it comes to you. I don't want him to hurt you."

"I'm a big girl; I can take care of myself."

"I know you think that, but I also know that you've always had a sweet spot for Devlin."

"That's not true."

"I saw it years ago—that night I brought him home from the bar. You were very concerned about him."

"Because I could see how drunk and sad he was, and you wouldn't tell me what was going on."

"That probably wasn't fair, but I didn't want rumors to get started, and I wasn't sure you could keep it to yourself."

"Well, that was all a long time ago. And you don't have to

be concerned. There's nothing going on between Devlin and me. We're just...friends." She felt a little depressed as she said the words, because despite her very recent speech to Devlin on the same topic, she didn't really want to just be friends, even though it was all they could be. "Speaking of friends," she said, changing the subject. "I didn't realize that you and Mom used to hang out with Claire and Graham. Devlin showed me a bunch of photos of the four of you together. When did that end?"

"When your mother and I started having problems. She didn't want anyone to see the strain between us, so we started saying no to invitations, and eventually the invitations stopped coming. After your mom left, I became a third wheel to Claire and Graham's love story, so I kept my distance."

"Until a few weeks ago when you and Claire had a very personal conversation."

"She needed someone to talk to, someone who had known her and Graham for a long time, and that was me. But the person she really wanted to speak to was Graham. That's what I told him. I don't regret saying it; I was trying to help. But Graham couldn't see that."

"Devlin gave his father an ultimatum. If he doesn't hire you back, then Devlin will quit."

"That won't do any good. Someone has to make good on our orders. I don't want Devlin throwing himself under the bus for me."

"I think he's doing it for himself, too. He needs his father to know that he's in charge."

"Graham doesn't react well to ultimatums. Devlin might find himself out on his ass."

"I hope not, but I wanted you to know that he's still trying, so maybe put off these interviews you've been scheduling."

"I'll think about it, but it might be time for me to move on."

She was surprised at his statement. "The Boatworks has been your whole life."

"And the past week I've begun to realize that might be the saddest thing of all."

"Really? I've never heard you talk like this."

"And you probably wish I'd had this epiphany a long time ago." He gave her a sad look. "I'm sorry for breaking up our family, Hannah. I don't know if I ever said that to you."

Her eyes blurred with tears. "I appreciate you saying it now, but I know there were two sides."

"There were. But my devotion to work was a big part of our problems. In retrospect, I realized I used work as an escape from the unhappiness I could feel in both your mother and me, and then it became the breaking point. I don't know how much you're working these days, Hannah, but I suspect your hours have gotten longer since your breakup with Gary."

"That might be true."

"Work is important, especially if you love it, if it brings you joy. But don't make my mistakes. Don't use your job as an escape or a hideout. The years go fast. You don't want to wake up one day and wonder what the hell you're doing and why you spent so much time caring about things that don't matter."

"Is that how you feel, Dad?"

"Today…a little bit."

"Is there anything I can do?"

"You're doing it. You're here. Want to share some rocky road ice cream with me?"

Considering she'd had cake at the party, she should probably say no, but she hadn't had this personal of a conversation with her dad since she was a teenager. "Sounds perfect."

CHAPTER ELEVEN

NOTHING WAS QUITE RIGHT, Devlin thought, as he drove down-town Saturday afternoon. It hadn't been right for the last three days, ever since he'd messed up his evening with Hannah.

Why had he kicked her out? Why had he jumped so far ahead? Why hadn't he just let himself enjoy her company?

He knew why. Because being with Hannah had put all kinds of bad ideas into his head, ideas that he didn't normally have about women. He preferred things simple, fun, uncomplicated. While Hannah might be fun, she was not simple or uncomplicated.

Unfortunately, kicking Hannah out had not put an end to his ideas. He hadn't been able to stop thinking about her. He'd looked for her and Frank out on the ocean, hoping to catch a glimpse of them in the *Daisy Mae*, but there had been no sign of them. And every time he saw a blonde walking along the street, he'd done a double-take. But, somehow, he'd made it to Saturday without seeing her. It seemed unbelievable. King Harbor wasn't that big. She had to be avoiding him.

Blowing out a frustrated breath, he wished he could take his restlessness out to the sea, but he'd promised to check in on his grandmother while his dad was out of town. He'd done that earlier in the day, and now he was headed to the Bickmore Hotel for tea with Fiona. He needed to put his tense emotions aside for at least the next few hours.

After parking behind the hotel, he met his grandmother in the grand lobby. The hotel décor was vintage luxury: gleaming hardwood floors, antique furniture, and art from the Roaring Twenties.

Fiona stood by the hostess station. She'd had her silvery-white hair styled, and she was looking happy in a soft pink floral dress.

"Right on time. I've always liked that about you, Devlin." She gave him a kiss on the cheek, then wiped off the smudge her bright-pink lipstick had left with a smile. "And I also like that you're willing to take your old grandmother to tea when I'm sure you'd rather be on the ocean."

"Not at all. I'm looking forward to this." He gave her his arm. "May I escort you in?"

"Yes, you may."

They were seated at a table by the window, overlooking the gardens. The tables were about half-full and most of the diners were women, with only a few men sprinkled in. He knew his father hated tea at the Bickmore, but it was something his grandmother and mother enjoyed quite a bit. His grandmother was no doubt missing his mother a great deal. During the summer months in King Harbor, they spent a lot of time together. He needed to make sure she wasn't lonely.

"I hope you like tea, Devlin," she said, with a twinkle in her eyes. "Or if you need a little kick in it, I have a flask in my purse."

"Nana. You should not be carrying around a flask."

"At my age, I can do anything I want."

"That must feel freeing."

She tilted her head, giving him a speculative look. "What don't you feel free to do?"

"Oh, I don't know. I didn't mean anything by my words."

"Words always mean something."

Fortunately, he didn't have to come up with a better answer, because the waitress was at their table. The older woman ran through their tea options in great detail. He'd had no idea there were so many variations of tea. When his grandmother ordered green jasmine tea, he did the same, hoping it would taste good. But his preference for a caffeinated hot beverage was coffee, black and strong, no sugar or cream.

"So, Devlin, how is it going at the Boatworks without your right-hand man?" his grandmother asked.

"Not well. News is getting out that Frank may be done, and I've had to talk two customers out of pulling their orders for new boats."

"Why don't you hire him back?"

"Because Dad fired him."

"Which was petty, but it's your company, Devlin."

"Under the umbrella of Blackthorne Enterprises. But I reminded Dad that he'd promised me autonomy. I threatened to quit if he isn't willing to hire Frank back."

"What happened?"

"He went back to Boston, and I don't have an answer."

"Your father can be quite contrary, you know. He's been that way since he was a little boy. If I told him I didn't want him to do something, he couldn't do anything else."

"I can't even picture Dad as a little boy."

"Well, he was just as stubborn and opinionated but a lot shorter," she said. "But your father also has a big heart and a soft side that he doesn't like to show. He thinks it will make him look weak. But it's still there, Devlin. He's very upset about your mother."

"Then why doesn't he talk to her?"

"I have a feeling he doesn't know what to say."

He shook his head. "I think it's more that he doesn't want to address her issues."

"Probably both. But you'll have to let your parents work out their own problems."

"Don't worry, I will. I have enough problems with my dad."

"Well, he's coming home tomorrow night. I spoke to him a short while ago."

"Good. Have you also spoken to my mother?"

"No. I've been hoping she'd contact me. I miss Claire. She's a daughter to me."

"I miss her, too. I've been trying to respect her need for space from all of us by not texting her or calling her, but I also worry that she'll think I don't care."

"She knows you care. She loves you, Devlin. She loves all of her kids, not just her sons, but also her nephews. This isn't about any of you. She turned sixty; she feels at a cross-roads. She's wondering how she's going to live the rest of her life, and my son has been a blind idiot. Hopefully, he will come to his senses, and they will both figure out how they can continue being happy together."

"I thought they were happy. Mom has always been a great complement to Dad. They were a good team. This threw me."

"It surprised all of us. But change can be good."

"I hope so." His eyes widened as the waitress set down a spectacular four-tiered tray filled with sandwiches, wraps, and sweets. "I didn't realize this was part of afternoon tea."

"I thought you'd like it."

As he waited for the waitress to pour his tea, his gaze caught on a trio of young women entering the room, especially the pretty blonde in the middle of the group. His heart thudded against his chest. He'd forgotten that Hannah had agreed to have tea with Jessica and Caroline today.

Hannah looked amazing in an off-the-shoulder floral dress, falling over her bare shoulders in beautiful waves. As the women were escorted through the room by the hostess, they passed by his table.

Hannah's blue eyes widened when she saw him. "Devlin," she said, coming to an abrupt stop. "I didn't expect to see you here."

He got to his feet, his smile encompassing all three women. "I got an invitation from a very special woman—my grandmother, Fiona Blackthorne. Nana, I think you've met some of these ladies before."

"Jessica and Caroline, yes," his grandmother said, then turned to Hannah with a quizzical look in her eyes. "I think I know you, too, dear."

"I'm Hannah Reid, Mrs. Blackthorne."

"Oh, my goodness, Hannah, of course. You're Frank's daughter. I remember you when you were a little girl."

"It's nice to see you again," Hannah said.

"You, too. I hope you'll give my regards to your dad, although I'm sure he's not too happy with any of us these days."

"I'll let him know you said hello. We better get to our table," Hannah added, giving him a quick look that couldn't mask the longing and uncertainty in her gaze.

He sucked in a breath, wondering if she knew just how much she'd revealed. But she quickly turned away and followed Caroline and Jessica to their table.

When he sat down and turned back to his grandmother, he had a feeling he'd just revealed too much as well.

"So, it's like that," she said with a knowing gleam.

"It's nothing."

"Oh, I think it's something."

"Hannah is furious with me that her father was fired."

"That might be, but the sparks I saw had nothing to do with anger."

"You are imagining things."

"And you are a terrible liar. What's Hannah like?" she asked with interest.

He thought about the best way to describe her. "She's

smart, bold, and pushy. She doesn't back down from a fight, not when she's fighting for someone she loves, that's for sure."

"I respect that in a person."

"I do, too."

"How long will she be in town?"

That was a loaded question. "Probably not long enough," he admitted.

Fiona gave him a soft smile. "Well, you might have to do something about that, Devlin. You're not getting any younger."

He laughed. "You did not just say that, Nana."

"Well, it's true. So, what are you going to do?"

"Nothing. Hannah lives in Austin, Texas. She's only staying in town long enough to sail with her father and try to beat me in the race."

"They're racing against you? Oh, my. Your father will not like that."

"I'm trying to use it as incentive to get Dad to race with me."

"That's an excellent plan. And it sounds to me like you have at least another week to convince Hannah to extend her stay."

"You mean uproot her entire life? It's not going to happen."

"It could happen. You know what I've always admired about you, Devlin? When you see what you want, you go after it. You can be relentless."

"I didn't say I wanted Hannah. I barely know her."

"But you know she's special. You should find out if there's something there that you want to fight for. The worst thing you can have in life is regret for missing an opportunity. I don't want you to regret anything. In the meantime, try the olive sandwich; it's amazing."

"Olive sandwich, huh?" He was happy with the change of

subject but not so excited about the mini-sandwich his grandmother was offering him.

"It's a tapenade. You'll love it. Have I ever steered you wrong?"

He laughed. "I guess you haven't."

"Then eat. Hannah is not going anywhere—at least not yet."

Hannah tried really hard not to turn her head, but out of the corner of her eye she could still see Devlin. She couldn't believe he was here. She'd been avoiding the docks and the Yacht Club for the last few days, so she wouldn't run into him, but she'd thought tea at the Bickmore was safe. But no, there he was, looking so handsome and sexy with his brown hair falling over his eyebrows and his expressive brown eyes that revealed far more than he probably knew. And to make him even more endearing, he was having tea with his grandmother. *How sweet was that?*

She picked up her cup and sipped her tea, focusing on Jessica and Caroline, who had been talking wedding dresses for the last ten minutes.

"I'm sorry," Caroline said suddenly, giving her an apologetic look. "This has to be boring for you, Hannah. I was just so excited to find the dress I wanted right here in town, at the only bridal boutique within a hundred miles. It was shocking. I thought for sure I'd have to go down to Boston or New York."

"It was meant to be."

"I think it was," Caroline agreed. "I've been feeling that way about a lot of things lately. It's like the universe is giving me sign after sign that I'm on the right path. Planning this wedding has been surprisingly easy."

"I don't think that's the universe," Jessica said dryly. "I've been helping."

"Oh, I know, but I was walking out of the bakery and saw the perfect dress in the window display. And then I crossed the street to put money in my meter, and I saw a flyer in the travel agency for a resort in Antigua, where I have always wanted to go, and they were featuring a honeymoon package for 50 percent off. How big a coincidence is that? What do you think, Hannah? Do you believe in signs? Or in fate?"

"Not really. I think we make our own destiny."

"I agree," Jessica said. "We all choose the lives we want to live. And even if we don't make a choice, that's a choice."

"That's true," Caroline said. "But sometimes there are signs, and we need to be receptive to them. If we keep going, with our heads down, never looking up or around, we'll miss them."

For some reason, Caroline's words resonated deep within her. She'd been on one path for a long time. Not even Gary had been a detour from that path. He'd been a real estate attorney. They'd talked a lot about properties and deals. He'd lined up perfectly with her life. But now she was here in King Harbor, nowhere she'd planned to be, and suddenly everything seemed up in the air.

Was she meant to go home and get back on the path? Or was it time to forge a new trail?

The questions ran around in her head as their conversation moved on to less thoughtful topics. Sipping tea and sharing crustless sandwiches and decadent scones with two girls she'd grown up with felt remarkably comfortable and pretty wonderful.

She had friends in Austin, but they weren't like these girls. They didn't remember her when she was a child. They didn't have stories to share about teachers and neighbors, and kids she'd grown up with. And those stories made her miss

King Harbor more, made her wish she could have stayed here instead of leaving with her mother.

However, it was pointless to go down that road. Her mother's choices had changed her life, and they hadn't all been bad. She'd longed to live with her dad, but her mother had done her best to fill that empty space. She'd been very attentive, and they'd been close through the years. But now she was starting to realize that she'd gone from living her father's life to living her mother's life. She probably would have lived Gary's life if he hadn't broken up with her. It was time to choose what she wanted for herself—all on her own.

She couldn't help noticing when Devlin and his grandmother left their table. Not just because he was no longer lurking in the corner of her eye, but because his grandmother's infectious laugh no longer flowed through the room.

She didn't know Fiona, but she'd always seemed like a sparkly and fun person. But then, all the Blackthornes were bigger than life. She'd always envied the family, not for their money or their power, but for all the love she'd seen between them.

The brothers and cousins had ruled King Harbor in her youth, and while they might have been wild boys, they'd also been good guys. They'd had tragedy in their lives. The cousins had lost their parents. The brothers had lost their aunt and uncle. But the kids had all been truly loved, which was certainly a tribute to Claire and Graham, as much as she didn't want to give Graham any credit.

As an only child, she'd wished desperately for a sibling, especially when her parents were fighting. It would have been great to have someone in the middle alongside her, someone she could talk to, who would understand what it felt like to watch your parents splitting apart. Thankfully, she'd had her girlfriends. It hadn't been the same, but it had definitely helped.

"This was great," Jessica said, as they paid their bill. "It's so nice to have you here, Hannah. You should come back more often."

"Definitely for my wedding at the end of summer," Caroline said.

"And for mine next fall," Jessica added.

"Looks like I'll be making a lot of trips here."

"Or you could just stay," Caroline suggested. "We have realty companies here, you know. And there are lots of new homes going up. King Harbor is even more popular than it used to be, so the prices are going up, up, and up."

"Something to think about," Jessica put in. "Real estate aside, we still have the incredible ocean in our backyard, and that's hard to beat."

"I will think about it. I've actually been feeling like a change would be good for me. But it's a big decision. Shall we go?"

They made their way out of the hotel, saying good-bye in the lobby, with hugs all around, and then Jessica and Caroline headed to their cars, while she decided to walk around the downtown before heading home. It was four o'clock now, and there were plenty of tourists out and about on a Saturday afternoon.

As her friends had said, King Harbor had definitely grown since she'd been a kid. There were more high-end boutiques, restaurants boasting both farm-to-table and sea-to-table selections, gourmet markets offering organic foods, gift shops, antiques, and a fabulous two-story bookstore with reading groups for both adults and kids. The Center Theater where Caroline worked was still in the town square but had seen a massive remodel, and next to it was a new Irish pub touting after-theater Irish coffees.

She meandered in and out of the stores for over an hour, enjoying the fact that there was so much more shopping now. If all these boutiques had been here a decade ago, her mother might have stayed.

When she saw the sign for Mendelson Realty, her steps slowed. There were a number of flyers on the display window, and she paused to look at a two-bedroom cottage located on the ocean bluff. Her pulse leapt. It was one of the houses she'd seen from Devlin's boat the other day. The diamond-paned windows glittered in the light, and the veranda with Adirondack chairs overlooking the sea, as well as the lush garden complete with a trickling rock waterfall, was right out of her dreams.

The price was pretty perfect, too. The description mentioned rustic charm, which probably meant the interior needed work, but that wasn't all bad if the bones of the house were good, as long as the location was as great as it appeared.

Was this a sign?

Caroline's words rang through her head. She'd said she didn't believe in fate or signs, but she could almost feel a hand on her back, urging her to go inside, get more information, maybe take a look at the house.

And then she saw another image in the window, the figure of a man right behind her. She whirled around, looking into Devlin's curious eyes.

"What are you doing here?" she asked, feeling breathless.

"I was at the hardware store." He tipped his head to the building across the street. "Didn't you hear me call your name?"

"No, I didn't. Where's your grandmother?"

"She went home. I had some errands to run. Did you have a nice time with your friends?"

"It was great to catch up. I'd forgotten how well we all got along."

"It looked like you were having a good time."

"It sounded like you were as well. Your grandmother has a very infectious laugh."

"That she does—sometimes fueled by the flask of Black-thorne Gold she keeps in her purse."

She smiled at the tender amusement in his eyes. "I didn't know that. However, you still must have been very entertaining."

"She actually finds herself quite amusing, too. But it was fun. So, what were you looking at that had you so captivated you couldn't hear me calling your name?" He moved around her to gaze at the flyer on the window. "One of your pretty hill houses."

"Yes. It caught my eye."

"Uh-oh, it says it's rustic. I know that's code for needs work."

"It is, but I'd kind of like to see it—for curiosity's sake," she added, not wanting him to get the wrong idea. "Not because I want to buy it. I'm curious as to how things have changed around here."

"Sure." There was a gleam in his eyes that told her he wasn't quite buying her explanation.

"It's true."

"Let's go in and find out more about it."

Before she could say no, he opened the front door and walked inside. She wondered what he'd do if she just left, but since she was interested in learning more, she reluctantly followed him into the office. He was already chatting it up with an older woman, who had platinum-blonde hair and was dressed in a crisp blue linen sheath dress.

Devlin broke away from his conversation. "Hannah, this is Kathy Lawrence, one of the best agents in town, and a friend of my mom's."

Of course he would know the real estate agent. She smiled at the other woman. "Hello, I'm Hannah Reid."

"Devlin says you're interested in the cottage on Pelican Drive."

"It looks very charming," she said. "Will it be open this weekend?"

"Yes, it will be open tomorrow, but I'm actually heading

up there in about twenty minutes; I have a client who wants to see it. If you're free, I can take you there now."

Was that another sign?

"I am free, but I should let you know I'm not a serious buyer. I grew up here and I always loved those houses on the hill. But I live in Austin now. I'm actually a real estate agent there."

"No problem, and your name is very familiar," Kathy said slowly. "Your mother is Marianne Reid?"

"She is."

"I remember her. We were in PTA together. I have a son—Rob—he was in Devlin's grade. Did you know him?"

"No, But I'm five years younger than Devlin."

"Of course. Anyway, I was sorry when your parents broke up. Your mom was always so good at running the Halloween fair."

"I forgot about that. She loved doing the haunted house."

"It was never the same after she left." Kathy checked her watch. "If you want to see the house before my client arrives, we should go now."

She wanted to say yes, then remembered… "Actually, I don't have a car. I walked into town."

"You and your walking," Devlin said with a laugh. "It's at least a three-mile walk from your house to here."

"It's good exercise." She turned back to Kathy. "Perhaps I can ride with you and then get a rideshare back from the house."

"You could do that," Kathy said.

"Or I could take you," Devlin put in. "I'd actually like to see the house."

"That will work." Kathy took her purse out of a drawer in her desk. "Let's go."

She wanted to protest, but Kathy was headed out the door, and Devlin was waving her forward, mentioning his car was right outside. A moment later, she slid into the passenger seat of his Audi.

"I'm starting to wonder if you drive around town looking for me, just so you can give me a ride," she said dryly.

He grinned. "It's just a happy coincidence."

"Is it happy? I thought we'd agreed to not hang out anymore."

"I don't remember that."

"You don't? Seriously?"

"We're friends, Hannah. Isn't that what we decided?"

"I suppose. Still, I can't believe you're that interested in looking at a house."

"You've made me curious about those hill houses. I might not want to live in my apartment forever."

"You said it was convenient."

"It has been, but as you told me, it can be good to have a break between work life and home life." He paused. "How's the *Daisy Mae* coming along? I heard you and your dad took her out yesterday."

"Who did you hear that from?"

"Donnie Blake. He's also entered in the race. He thinks both Frank and I are going to lose now that we've split up."

"I guess that's possible. But you have a better chance of losing."

He shot her a grin. "I love your confidence, even if it's misplaced."

She knew it probably was misplaced, but she wasn't going to tell him that. "Have you found your racing partner yet?"

"My dad will be home tomorrow. I'll get his final answer —on everything."

She took a quick breath at that piece of information. She only wanted a final answer if it was in the affirmative. If it wasn't, she didn't know what her dad would do.

"I hope your dad has come to his senses," she said. "But it might be too late. My father went to Portland today."

Devlin hit the brakes hard, and she braced her hand against the dashboard. "Whoa."

"Sorry. I didn't think Kathy was going to stop on the yellow light."

"Was that it or were you rattled to know that my dad is talking to Victory Sailing, one of your biggest competitors?"

"I thought Frank would give me more time. I'm trying to make things right."

"I know you are, Devlin, but at the end of the day, even if you throw yourself under the bus, my dad might still get run over. He has to look out for himself."

"Is that what you told him?"

"No. I actually suggested that he give you more time."

His gaze softened. "Seriously? Why?"

"There are a lot of reasons. My dad loves the Boatworks and his job. But mostly it's because you're a good man, Devlin. You've put your own job on the line for him, and that's amazing."

"I'm glad you think so." He gave her a look so long that the car behind them sounded the horn. He hastily drove through the intersection.

She turned her gaze out the window, afraid she'd revealed far too much.

CHAPTER TWELVE

DEVLIN HAD ONLY OFFERED to take Hannah to see the house because he wanted to spend time with her, but he had to admit the cottage was something special. The bathrooms were old and needed work, but the second-floor master suite was impressive, and the ocean views from three sides of the house were spectacular. There was also a rooftop deck with a telescope set up. Clearly, the night sky was as compelling as the ocean.

As he followed Hannah and Kathy around the house, he only half-listened to their conversation. Occasionally, he smiled to himself, because it was obvious that Hannah was trying to act as if this visit was nothing more than professional curiosity, but he'd seen the wonder in her eyes when she'd first stepped across the threshold, when she'd entered the master bedroom, and wandered out on the deck.

She was falling in love with the house.

But where would that lead? Would she really move back here? Or was this house going to be another sad memory of what she'd left behind in King Harbor?

When they made their way downstairs and onto the front

deck, Kathy left them alone while she moved inside to take a phone call.

"What do you think?" he asked, as they stood at the rail, looking out at the water.

"It's beautiful," she murmured, turning her gaze to him.

He thought she was damn beautiful, too—her blonde hair lit with gold in the sunlight, her blue eyes alive with wonder and excitement.

"What's your opinion, Devlin?"

"I like the house. It feels like a home. I could see you living here."

"Really?"

"Yes. It's uniquely charming, and you can't beat this view."

"You have the same view at your apartment."

"Not quite as good as this."

"Maybe you should buy the house."

"Or you should," he countered.

She licked her lips. "What would I do with a house in King Harbor?"

"Live in it. You said you've missed the town and that you're at a crossroads in your work life. Why not make a change? Your dad lives here. You have friends here."

"My dad might leave if he decides to take a job elsewhere."

He hated the reminder that her father was currently interviewing with one of his competitors. He'd let the situation linger too long. He'd told himself that he was doing what he could to make peace between the two men, that Frank had some skin in the game, too, because he'd chosen to criticize Graham. He'd convinced himself that it wasn't all his dad's fault, but that wasn't true. This situation was completely on his father, and he shouldn't have given him more than a week to come to his senses.

"Devlin?" Hannah said, a question in her eyes. "Where

did you go? You got quiet."

"I'm sorry, Hannah. I should have resolved this situation with your dad before this."

"I know it's complicated."

"It got more complicated when my mom left. I had every intention of getting my father to rehire Frank before that. But he was so rattled by her leaving, I didn't push as hard as I should have. I gave him an ultimatum, but I didn't follow up on it. I should have. Tomorrow, I will tell him that time's up. Frank comes back, or I walk."

"What if he lets you go? What would you do?"

"I'd do what I'm doing now. I'd start my own company and work it from the ground up. It would be smaller. It would take me years to get to where I am now, but it would be mine."

"I'm sure it would be successful."

He appreciated her confidence in him. "It would be, or it wouldn't be, but either way, it would be a challenge, and I like challenges." He paused, wanting her to understand. "I grew up as a member of a powerful, successful family. There were a lot of expectations, most of which I didn't choose to fulfill. I didn't go to Harvard like most of my brothers. I didn't want to work in the whisky business. I didn't want to live in Boston. I said no so many times that when I finally took over the Boatworks, I felt like I needed to say yes to my father being involved on a limited basis. It wasn't difficult, because for the most part, he stayed out of the business. When this situation happened with Frank, I was thrown. I thought I had to respect my father's decision, because he's ultimately my boss, but his decision wasn't worthy of my respect. Anyway, it's difficult to explain, but—"

"I get it, Devlin. I don't know what it was like to grow up a Blackthorne, but I did go into business with my mother. She's my boss, and I know how it feels to try to forge your own way, without disrespecting your parent. I also realize that your mother's departure created chaos and uncertainty. My father's part in her departure didn't help."

"You're letting me off the hook?"

"We both know I let you off the hook awhile ago," she said with a smile. "But I'm still going to beat you in the race. I won't go easy on you, and you can't go easy on me."

"You don't have to worry about that. I always play to win. And since we're having an honest moment here, what do you really think of this house?"

"That it's pretty close to perfect, even though it needs attention. In my head, I can see exactly how it would look with the right furniture, new paint on the walls and colorful tile in the bathrooms. It would be amazing." She let out a breath. "I just wish it was in Austin."

"If it was, it wouldn't be amazing, because there would be no ocean view."

"I know." She paused as they heard a car door close. "I think Kathy's client is here. We should go—let them walk through the house on their own."

"All right." They slipped down the stairs, giving Kathy a wave before getting into his car.

As they drove away, he saw Hannah cast a longing look at the house.

"I hope those people don't make an offer," he said.

"Why?" she asked, her gaze moving back to his.

"It will give you time to think about it."

"I don't need time, Devlin. I have a life somewhere else. And in a week, I'll be back to it."

"Well, a lot can happen in a week."

A lot had already happened, Hannah thought as they drove away from her dream house. She'd reconnected with her dad, her friends, and Devlin. She'd found herself feeling inexplicably happy just being back in King Harbor. It felt like she belonged here.

She tried to tell herself it wouldn't last, that it was only the newness of her return, the fun of revisiting the past. Her future was in Austin—*wasn't it?*

She'd put a lot of time and effort into building a career there, and her mom would be terribly disappointed if she left. Although, her parents had both had a chance to pursue their dreams. *Why shouldn't she?*

Because dreams didn't last. The morning always came.

"Do you need to get home?" Devlin asked.

His question interrupted her depressing thoughts. "Not really. Why?"

"A friend of mine, one of my employees actually, has a pop-up pizza company that he operates out of a food truck on Friday and Saturday nights. It's probably the best pizza you'll ever eat."

"That's quite an endorsement."

"I speak the truth. But you can find out for yourself, unless you're still full after tea?"

She checked her watch, realizing it was already half past five. "Those little sandwiches seem like a long time ago now. I'd be up for pizza."

"Great. He's parked in the lot by Cooper's Beach tonight."

Devlin turned the car around and headed away from the downtown to a popular surfing beach on the outskirts of King Harbor. Cooper's Beach had the biggest waves for twenty miles and was always busy in the mornings and late afternoons, especially once they got past Memorial Day.

"Did you ever surf here?" she asked Devlin, as the ocean came into view.

"Years ago, when I was a teenager. I prefer sailing now. I don't like waiting for a wave. I like to make my own," he said with a charming grin. "What about you?"

"Sailing is also my favorite activity on the water."

"A girl after my own heart."

She smiled, but his words reminded her that his heart wasn't really available. She didn't know if he was still in love with his college girlfriend. But she did know that he'd put his heart on ice after her death and that he'd never had another serious relationship since then. Not only had he told her that, but Jessica and Caroline had been happy to relate how very single Devlin was, despite the fact that most of the single women in town would have been happy to date him.

She would have been happy to date him, too, if she lived here permanently, and if he didn't have a ghost for a first love. *Who could ever compete with that?*

She'd already lost her last fiancé to an ex; she wasn't about to fall for someone who was still in love with another woman. Which was why she should have turned down the pizza invitation, why she should be turning down every invitation that Devlin gave her.

On the other hand, as long as she knew what was what, why not have some fun?

She would only be here for another week. There was a definitive end coming, so maybe she should relax and enjoy herself.

Devlin parked in a fairly crowded lot by the beach. The days were getting longer, and sunset was at least two hours away. Not only were there plenty of surfers and beachgoers coming out of the ocean and off the sand, but there also appeared to be quite a few people who'd come just for pizza.

The food truck was parked near the picnic area, and most of the tables were full. There were also people perched along the low brick wall that ran around the parking lot.

She followed Devlin over to the truck, where they got into line.

"Your friend is popular," she said, her stomach rumbling at the delicious aroma of garlic, onions, sausage, and other Italian spices.

"I told you. What kind of pizza do you want? I'm thinking we should get half and half."

"Great. You know what's good, so you pick."

"Anything you hate?"

"Not a thing."

"Then why don't you grab us a table while I order?"

"Good idea." She stepped out of line and snagged a picnic table deep in a canopy of trees, but she could still see the water. While she was waiting for Devlin, she checked her phone and saw a text from her mom. She wanted to know if she could change her plans and come back for Memorial Day weekend, because she needed another person for an open house that had just come up on a three-million-dollar home. It would be a big commission for the company, and she wanted Hannah on it.

Despite the financial enticement, the last thing she wanted to do was go back to Austin to sit on an open house. In fact, it was her least favorite thing to ever do. She liked working with clients and taking them to homes on appointment, because it was personal and purposeful, but standing in an empty house on the off chance that someone other than a curious neighbor would come by was not interesting at all and usually a huge waste of time.

She texted: *Sorry, but Dad and I are going to race together, so I won't be back until the following week.*

Her mom's reply was not happy: *It's a boat race. This is your future, Hannah. I'm sure your dad will understand that work is more important. He should know that better than anyone.*

Her mother couldn't resist getting a dig in.

I need this, she typed.

I need you, her mom replied. *You know I have big plans for expanding the agency and you're a part of those plans, but you have to be committed. One day this business will be yours. I'm doing this for you.*

She stared at the text for a long minute. Her mom had been talking about her plans for the better part of a year, and she'd always thought she was committed, but after Gary had pulled the rug out from under her, everything she'd believed in had started to shift. For the past six months, she'd been questioning all her decisions, and those questions had amped up since she'd come to King Harbor.

In fact, she thought those questions were partly why she'd rushed across the country to see her dad. His firing had given her a reason to leave, to step out of her structured life and get more perspective. She certainly had a different view now. But she didn't know what to do with it.

She was only sure of one thing, so she sent back her answer. *I won't be able to help you with this open house. I've committed to this race and to Dad. I'll be home after that.*

I hope your father is not putting ideas in your head, her mother answered. *Our lives are here, Hannah. This isn't just my business; it's yours, too.*

I love you, Mom; I'll talk to you soon.

She didn't know if her mother would be satisfied with that, but she hoped so. She turned her phone over as Devlin set down a large pizza. One half was loaded with brightly colored vegetables, the other with sausage, pepperoni, peppers, and onions.

"That's a lot of pizza," she said with a laugh.

"Victor doesn't believe in small sizes. We can take whatever we don't eat home." He paused as her phone vibrated on the table.

She sighed and picked it up again, reading her mom's short answer: *I love you, too, but I'm disappointed. I thought you'd be thrilled we got this listing. I'll have to give it to Brandon if you won't be here.*

I understand, but I can't be there. Sorry.

She set her phone down again.

"Everything okay?" Devlin asked, his gaze thoughtful.

"Are you texting with your dad?"

"No, my mother. She wants me to come home for an open house Memorial Day weekend, and I told her that I'm committed to the race. She feels that shows a lack of commitment to her company, which she insists is all about providing for me and my future. But that's not completely true. She loves real estate, and she is very good at it. She'd be driven to make it as successful as possible even if I wasn't involved at all."

"Do you think she's jealous that you're choosing to spend more time with your dad?"

"Probably," she admitted. "I think she preferred it when we let our relationship slide. She doesn't like that I rushed to my dad's side. She's worried I'm forgetting that my dad let us down. She doesn't want me to turn him into the hero she doesn't believe he is."

"But you're not doing that, are you?" he asked, taking a bite of the veggie pizza.

"No, I'm not. I'm very aware that he allowed our family to break apart. It still stings that he didn't love us more than he loved his job. But I'm an adult now and I can recognize that it wasn't that simple. Their relationship was far more complicated than love versus work. I love my father, and I want him to be happy. I feel the same way for my mom. I don't want to take sides anymore. I don't want to feel like it's a competition."

"I completely agree."

"Are you taking sides in your parents' separation?" she asked curiously.

"No, because I don't know what the sides are. Except for my mother's dramatic exit speech, I know nothing about her problems with my dad, and my father is not inclined to fill me in. He says their marriage is between them."

"That's true. It took me a long time to learn that. I kept thinking I could fix them, but I couldn't."

"No, you couldn't. If I had to pick a side, it would be my mom's," he continued. "Because I know my dad can be a stubborn hard-ass."

"Your mom always seemed so sweet to me."

"She's a kind person, very generous, and I guess we all took her for granted, especially my dad. But hopefully they'll be able to work it out. I do think they're good for each other. Anyway, enough about family. Let's eat."

She was happy to end the conversation, because her mom's texts had hit her on a deeper level than they should have. Committing to the agency, to a future of more of the same, didn't sound good at all. Thankfully, she didn't have to deal with it for at least another week.

As she ate, she realized that the pizza more than lived up to Devlin's praise.

It was cheesy and flavorful, each bite a perfect delight, and she managed to get through two large slices without any trouble. She washed her food down with the ice-cold beer that Devlin had also brought to the table. "That was great," she said, wiping her mouth with a napkin.

"I wasn't sure on the beer choice, but he didn't have any wine."

"Beer was just right." She glanced around, the sound of laughter under a twilight sky making her feel so carefree. "Living here is like being on vacation all the time."

"That's why I stay."

"You have a lot of friends here." At least a dozen people had waved or greeted Devlin on their way past the table.

"It's a boating town; I've worked with a lot of the locals."

"And your family runs half the town."

"That, too." He paused, his gaze moving back toward the food truck. "Speaking of family, I guess not everyone left King Harbor…"

"What does that mean?" she asked, but he was already walking away from the table.

CHAPTER THIRTEEN

HANNAH WATCHED as Devlin greeted a tall, attractive, dark-haired man—another Blackthorne, but she couldn't quite place him. A moment later, they were heading in her direction.

"Hannah, this is my cousin, Jason."

She stood up to shake Jason's hand. "I'm Hannah Reid. I think we met years ago."

"Then it's nice to see you again. Is this pizza up for grabs?" he asked, sliding onto the bench across from her. "The line is really long."

"I'm done," she said, as she took her seat.

"It's all yours, Jason," Devlin added, sitting next to his cousin. "I didn't know you were back in town."

"I got in today. I'm going to be scouting locations this week."

"Locations?" she murmured. "Oh, wait, you're the filmmaker."

"Right now, I'm concentrating on television."

"Jason's first TV series, *Bad Intentions*, just started airing," Devlin said, a proud note in his voice. "The first episode was amazing."

"I'll have to check it out."

"And now we're starting to film season two," Jason put in, devouring his pizza in big, hungry bites.

"It must be exciting for you to see your vision come to life," she commented.

"It is, but I have to make sure season two is even better. The pressure is on. Not only from the public, but also from the family. Uncle Graham is giving me headaches about making sure Blackthorne Entertainment lives up to the Blackthorne brand," Jason added, exchanging a commiserating look with Devlin.

"I know what that feels like," Devlin agreed.

"But I work in Hollywood. It's not always that easy to control the message." Jason paused as his phone buzzed. Glancing at the screen, he said, "I gotta take this."

He left the table, moving under the trees to answer his call.

"So, that's Jason," Devlin said with a laugh. "These days, we get about ten words in between his phone calls."

"Another Blackthorne workaholic."

"We do love our work. My father and Jason's dad definitely instilled a strong work ethic in all of us. And because we've gone into different parts of the business, there is competitive pressure to be successful."

"Is it more difficult for your cousins? Do they ever feel like they're not quite in the mix?"

"I hope not, because I consider my cousins my brothers. After my aunt and uncle died in that plane crash, Phillip, Jason, and Brock came to live with us, and my parents always tried to make us feel like we were one family."

"Where is Jason in the lineup of cousins?"

"He's the middle child. And he definitely has that middle kid need to prove himself, make himself visible. I can't fault him, either, because we tended to lose Jason when we were out somewhere. We'd get to the car and be ready to pull out of the parking lot, and then someone would say, 'Where's Jason?' and we'd realize he was missing."

"He doesn't seem that invisible now." She tipped her head toward his animated conversation. "He has a lot of energy. You're much more chill."

"You think so, huh?"

"I do. You're passionate about boats and work, but I think you also value fun and maybe a slower pace. That's why you like King Harbor. It's not just that the town is on the ocean, it's also that it's a close community. Here you have an even bigger family."

"That's all true, especially the part about fun. That's important." He gave her a sexy smile that sent tingles of desire down her spine. "We could have a lot of fun together, Hannah."

She didn't know what to say to that. Every possible answer seemed a little dangerous. Thankfully, Jason returned to the table.

"I have to go," Jason said. "I'll catch up with you later, Dev. Hannah, I hope to see you again."

"I hope that as well."

"Are you staying in town?" Devlin asked.

"I'll be in and out, but I'm planning to be here for the race."

"You could sail with me. I'm still looking for a teammate."

"Nana can sail better than me," Jason said with a laugh. "You do not want me on your boat, but I will be cheering you on."

As Jason took off, Devlin said, "Want to walk down to the beach?"

"Sure."

Since Jason had finished what was left of their pizza, they tossed their trash into a can and then headed to the beach. Once on the sand, she kicked off her sandals. She loved to walk and adding in the beach just made it that much better. They strolled along the water's edge for over a mile.

"This is the perfect after-dinner walk," she said.

"I agree."

"Tell me about your travels, Devlin. You said you went all around the world?"

"For over two years. It was an amazing time. I saw some of the most beautiful places on earth."

"What was your favorite?"

"I had many favorites, but the small Caribbean island of Anguilla was pretty special. The sand was white, the water a clear turquoise blue, and the music at night was a sultry mix of reggae and pop."

"Sounds beautiful and romantic. Did you have a girl in every port, or maybe there was another woman on the crew?"

"There were a few women—not in every port. I wasn't that popular."

She made a face at his teasing smile. "I think you probably were."

"I had a good time. Although, working with some of the passengers was not that enjoyable. There were a lot of rich, entitled people on that yacht."

"You're rich and entitled."

"My family is rich, not me, and I certainly hope I have never acted that entitled."

"I'm sure you haven't. You're not a pretentious person."

He stopped walking. "Wait, was that a compliment?"

"Don't let it go to your head." She let out a wistful sigh as they continued on. "I do envy you, Devlin. You've done so much more than me. I've barely gone anywhere."

"Your life isn't over yet. If you want to travel, do it."

"You make it sound so simple."

"Maybe it is that simple."

He had a point. She did tend to complicate things. And after her broken engagement, she'd felt like she was in a holding pattern. She couldn't go forward, and she couldn't go back. She'd kept telling herself that she'd make changes sometime.

What was she waiting for?

Her life was happening right now—for better or worse. She wanted it to be better.

As day turned to twilight, they turned around and headed back to the parking lot, but she didn't move too fast. The starry sky and Devlin's presence made her want to linger on this beach forever. At one point, she stumbled in the sand, and Devlin slipped his hand into hers, leaving it there for the rest of their journey back.

When they reached the parking lot, it was almost nine o'clock. The food truck was gone, and with the exception of a group of six friends sitting at a picnic table, everyone else had vanished.

She was sorry to see the night end. It had been so much fun spending time with Devlin, getting to know him beyond the man who'd fired her father and the boy she'd crushed on as a teenager.

They were both quiet on the drive home, and the silence seemed to grow more tense with each passing mile. When Devlin pulled into the driveway of her father's house and shut off the engine, she felt like her nerves were screaming. She knew she needed to say goodnight and get out of the car, but she couldn't seem to move.

"I'll walk you to the door," Devlin offered.

"No. Let's say goodnight here." If he came to the door, she'd be tempted to invite him in, especially since her father wouldn't be back until tomorrow.

"Okay. I had fun, Hannah. I like spending time with you."

"I feel the same way."

He leaned over and gave her a kiss—a slow, hot, inviting kiss that sent butterflies through her stomach and made her body yearn for a lot more.

When he pulled away, she licked her lips, thinking about going in for another kiss, but that would take them down a road she was trying not to go.

She forced herself to open the car door and get out. Then she walked into her house and let out a frustrated breath. A moment later, she heard his engine fire up, and then there was nothing but silence. He was gone.

She should be happy, but she wasn't.

The long, lonely night loomed in front of her.

Devlin slammed into his apartment, annoyed with himself for kissing Hannah and then letting her go. That kiss had whetted his appetite, and now he had the whole damn night to think about it. But he had let her walk away. She wanted more than he had to give. He knew that deep down in his gut.

And maybe...just maybe he wanted more, too. Was that the real reason he'd let her go?

He hadn't felt such a strong connection to anyone in a very long time. He liked talking to Hannah, laughing with her, eating pizza together, walking on the beach, looking through her dream house. It didn't matter what they were doing; it was just good because she was there.

She was sharp and funny but also soft and vulnerable. She had a big, fierce, loyal heart, but it was also a heart that could be broken. And she'd already had a lot of pain in her life. He didn't want to bring her more.

Was it really her he was worried about or was it himself?

Since Amy's death, he had turned away from intense emotion. He had chosen to live a life that was easy and light and never too dark or too serious. Love could be all of those things, and he didn't do love anymore.

Why was he even thinking about love?

He stepped onto the deck and took several deep breaths.

He should do something productive, go downstairs and do some work, take his mind off Hannah. But he couldn't seem to generate any energy for that idea.

He could go to the estate, see if Jason was around, or his grandmother, but he didn't know if he was in the mood to deal with either of them. His grandmother would see too much, ask too many questions, and Jason would probably be on his phone half the night.

Turning away from the rail, he walked back into the house, thinking he might just go to bed so the night would be over sooner.

And then the doorbell rang.

His body tightened. It was probably Jason. Or maybe his father had come home early.

He pressed the intercom. "Yes?"

"It's me," Hannah said. "I need to talk to you."

His heart jumped into his chest. She was the last person he'd expected to ring his bell. "Come on up." He buzzed her in and then opened the front door.

She came down the hall a few minutes later, a gleam of steel fire in her eyes. He didn't know why she was angry, but something had obviously happened.

"What's wrong, Hannah?"

"Saying good night to you felt wrong."

Her words stunned him, stealing the breath from his chest.

Hannah lifted her chin, put her hands on his shoulders and looked him straight in the eye. "I keep putting myself on hold. I keep waiting for another day, a better time, a good reason, and I don't want to do it anymore. We have insane chemistry together, Devlin. I've been fighting it hard, but I don't want to fight it anymore. I want you."

"Are you sure?" He didn't know why he was giving her a chance to change her mind. But he couldn't quite believe what she was saying.

Her gaze didn't waver. "Positive. You don't have to worry.

I'm not looking for anything more than tonight. Just one night —you and me. I want to make it simple."

"But you don't do simple," he reminded her. "You told me you like to complicate things."

"I want to change. I want to live in the moment. You're not going to say no, are you?" she asked, a worried gleam coming into her gaze.

"Do you think I'm crazy?"

She smiled. "No, but I think you're incredibly hot, and I'd really like to see what's under those clothes."

"Right back at you. I guess you should come in."

"Oh, I am definitely coming in." She gripped his shoulders more tightly as she stood on her tiptoes, pressing her mouth against his.

He let her take the lead, loving the mix of shyness and boldness in her kiss.

But she was going too slow, and his desire was sending the blood roaring through his veins. When she let out a sigh of pleasure, it completely undid him.

He pulled her into his apartment and backed her up against the wall, kissing her with a hunger that had been building inside him for days. Her mouth was so sexy, so sweet, but he wanted more. He pulled her hair to one side, as he slid his lips down the side of her neck, eliciting more murmurs of pleasure, and he felt the same joy as he ran his hands over her soft curves. But he couldn't take Hannah against the wall. He wanted a bed. He wanted soft pillows underneath her head. He wanted to take his time, touch and taste every inch of her.

"Bedroom," he somehow managed to get out. He grabbed her hand, pulling her across the room. Only it took too long, and he had to steal a kiss in the hallway and another as they entered the room. She laughed as they bumped into the dresser.

"Don't kill me on the way, Devlin."

He grinned. "If I don't get you out of that dress soon, I'm going to die."

"We don't want that."

She turned around, and he gripped her zipper with a greedy hand, pulling it down to her lower back, touching his lips to her spine and then spinning her back around.

She stepped out of her dress, and it pooled on the floor. As she stood in front of him in a lacy white bra and lavender panties, his body went hard. She then took off her bra and tossed it onto his shoulder, and he couldn't look anywhere else but her soft full breasts.

He cupped her breasts with his hands and then lowered his head, tasting one pink nipple and then the other.

"Oh, God, now I'm going to die," she said breathlessly. "You're torturing me."

"Not even close," he said, lifting his gaze back to hers. "I have lots of fun in store for you." He laughed as her blue eyes blazed with fire. "I can see you like that idea."

"Very much." She gave him a cheeky smile. "But first, let's see what's under your shirt." Her fingers ripped apart his buttons with impatience and desire.

He then shrugged the shirt off, appreciating the look of pleasure in her eyes.

"Wow," she murmured. "Tan, fit, abs to die for, sexy as hell. How did I get this lucky?"

"I'm the lucky one." He pulled her against him and kissed her once more, slipping his tongue past her parted lips, as her breasts brushed his chest. They kissed for long minutes as desire spun them around and around, until he felt trapped in the web that was Hannah.

And then her hand was on the snap of his jeans, and he sucked in a quick breath, as he pulled his mouth from hers. He stepped back and took off his jeans and briefs. Then he helped her slide her panties down her curvy hips. With her beautiful naked body in front of him, he fell to his knees, his hands on her waist, his mouth on her hot core.

She murmured his name, running her hands through his hair. He could feel her tremble, and he wanted to take her as high as she'd ever been. He touched her and tasted her until she gasped for pleasure and collapsed against him. Then he picked her up and took her to the bed, gently placing her on the mattress. Reaching into his nightstand, he pulled out a condom.

She smiled. "Glad you remembered that. I actually did bring one, but I have no idea where it is right now."

"Don't worry, I have plenty."

"You're confident."

"Oh, I am."

She helped him put on the condom with fumbling and endearing fingers and then fell back against the pillows, pulling him on top of her. "I want you, Devlin."

"Not as much as I want you," he returned, feeling an overwhelming wave of desire and need.

He didn't know what tomorrow would bring, but tonight was theirs, and he was going to make it a night to remember.

Hannah slipped out of bed early Sunday morning, taking one last look at Devlin's handsome form before she left. He was sprawled on his stomach, his hair tousled from her hands and from sleep, a shadow of beard on his jaw, the sheet barely covering his very fine ass.

The knot in her stomach tightened as memories of their night together ran through her. She wanted to crawl back into bed and snuggle up next to him. She wanted to touch him and kiss him again, making love the way they had two times already.

But she'd promised him and herself that it was just for a night.

And the night was over.

She put on her clothes, trying to be as quiet as possible, because if he woke up, if he asked her to stay, she didn't see how she could possibly say no. She had to leave now—before it was too late.

Although, she had the somewhat desperate thought that it might already be too late, that her feelings for Devlin might be about as far from simple as they could get.

When she entered the living room, she thought about leaving a note. *But what would she say?* She'd said it all with her actions. Words would only add complications that neither of them wanted.

She slipped out the front door and jogged down the steps. Fortunately, no one was at work yet to see her walk of shame. Once outside, she headed toward her dad's house, which was only a few blocks away. It felt good to be outside, to feel the rising sun on her head, to see the sparkling blue of the ocean.

She felt both happy and a little sad. She loved King Harbor. It was going to be hard to say good-bye—not only to the city but also to the man she'd left sleeping in his very comfortable king-sized bed.

Being with Devlin had felt absolutely right. The chemistry between them was off the charts, but it was the emotional connection that had surprised her. They'd been completely in sync in every way. And it hadn't all been about sex; it had also been about laughter, joy, talking into the dark hours of the night, falling asleep in each other's arms.

Dammit, she silently swore.

She wasn't supposed to fall for him.

It was just a fling, a one-night stand—light, easy, breezy —but she already wanted another night.

Maybe she could have one…she wasn't leaving for a few more days.

Two nights could still be a fling—even three. Four might be pushing it. Five definitely too much.

Oh, who was she kidding? If she went back to Devlin again, she'd probably never find the strength to leave. It would never be enough.

Wanting to outrun her turbulent thoughts, she jogged the rest of the way home. When she entered the house, she was surprised to hear her father's voice. She hadn't thought he would be home from Portland until the afternoon.

He came down the hallway, a concerned look in his eyes. "Where have you been? It's barely seven."

She suddenly felt like a teenager caught after curfew and felt her cheeks flushing with heat.

Her father's gaze narrowed. "Devlin?"

She was an adult. She didn't have to explain or apologize, but she found herself wanting to do both.

"Forget it. You don't have to tell me," he said quickly.

"I didn't think you'd be home so early."

"I don't sleep well in hotels. I left at five."

"What happened at the interview?"

"They made it clear they'd like to have me on board."

"What did you say?"

"That I had to think about it."

She could see the stress in his eyes and in the weary lines across his weathered face. He'd aged five years since he'd lost his job. "Would you really leave King Harbor? It has been your home forever. You swore you'd never leave."

"I know I did, but things are different now."

"Devlin still wants you back. His father is coming home today. He's going to talk to him again. He will put his career on the line for you."

"I never asked him to do that."

"That's who he is. He believes in you."

"And he wants to stand up to his father."

"That, too," she admitted. "But it's still a big gesture."

Her father gave her a tired smile. "You are sweet on him."

"He's a good person. I know you've always thought so, too. When do you have to decide, Dad?"

"Not for a few days. Do you want breakfast? I was going to make some pancakes."

"That sounds great."

They moved into the kitchen, and she slid onto a stool at the island while her dad pulled out a griddle and set it on the stove.

"What are you going to do today?" she asked.

"Work on the *Daisy Mae*. I picked up some parts I needed in Portland yesterday. I'd like to get her in the water tomorrow, Tuesday at the latest."

"That would be good. We need to start practicing. I'm not worried about you, but my skills could use some work."

"We have time." He paused, as he gave her a worried look. "I hope you're being careful, Hannah. With your heart," he added awkwardly. "I like Devlin, but I've never seen him in a relationship."

"I know what I'm doing. And if my heart gets broken, that's okay. Because it means I'm taking risks; I'm living life. It's better than never taking a chance because I'm afraid of getting hurt, right?"

"I suppose. I know your mother and I haven't been the best example for a long-term relationship."

"I think you could have fought harder to keep Mom," she said honestly. "But I wasn't in your marriage, so what do I know?"

"You're right. I could have fought harder, but I think in the end we still would have split up, because we didn't work together. My biggest regret was hurting you and losing you."

"You haven't lost me. I'm here now."

He walked around the counter and gave her a hug. "I'm very glad you came home. Can I give you one small piece of wisdom?"

"You can," she said warily.

"It's love that matters, Hannah. In the end, that's all it's about. You can strive for fortune and fame, but at the end of the day, it's who you love and who loves you. Don't follow in my footsteps or even in your mother's. We both made a lot of mistakes. Learn from us what *not* to do."

She felt tears come to her eyes. He'd never spoken such deep and emotional words. She gave him a teary smile. "You did a lot of things right, too, Dad. I don't think I gave you enough credit."

"I'm sure your mother thinks you gave me too much."

"Probably."

He smiled. "I'll say one thing—you've always been very honest. You are the best thing your mother and I ever did together."

"And I love you both."

"Do you also love Devlin?"

"Oh, Dad…"

"I know. It's none of my business."

"We're having fun. It's not serious. It doesn't mean anything, and I'm sorry if that makes you uncomfortable, but you said you appreciated my candor."

"I just hope you're being honest with yourself. Sometimes we force ourselves to believe the lie, because the truth is too difficult."

CHAPTER FOURTEEN

IT WAS HARD NOT to call Hannah, not to try to see her. But after waking up alone on Sunday morning, Devlin realized that she'd made good on her promise of one night only. He should have been happy about that. Awkward morning-after conversations were his least favorite thing in the world. She'd saved him from that.

But as the hours passed, as Sunday turned in to Monday, he'd broken down and texted her.

Her answer had been short, making it clear she was fine with their very short fling, while he clearly was not. But he hadn't let on. He'd played the game her way. Then he'd tried to distract himself with work, telling himself he would eventually forget her. That hadn't worked particularly well.

Now it was Tuesday afternoon, and he was going to try to distract himself with a practice run. If the ocean didn't keep his mind off Hannah, his father probably would.

As he paced around the deck of the *Wind Warrior*, he wished his father would show up already. His dad was supposed to have come back on Sunday, then it was Monday, now it was today. He still wasn't sure that his father would actually get on the boat, but he'd promised to go for a sail with him, and usually his dad didn't break his promises.

They needed this sail for a lot of reasons. He needed to get Frank back to work, and he hoped to get his dad to agree to race with him. He was running out of time on every front.

He stiffened as he saw Hannah come down the dock. She stopped abruptly when her gaze caught his, and in that unguarded moment, the memories they'd shared sizzled between them like a live electrical wire.

He'd been crazy to think he was going to forget about her any time soon.

He moved down the stairs. "Hello, Hannah."

"Hi, Devlin," she said, wariness in her eyes. "Are you taking your boat out or did you just get in?"

"I'm taking it out as soon as my dad gets here. We're going to have our long-anticipated conversation. He finally came back from Boston late last night."

"That's good."

"I hope it's good. We'll see. What about you?"

"My father and I are going to test out the *Daisy Mae*." She crossed her fingers for luck.

He smiled. "Hannah."

"Devlin?"

"I've missed you."

Her gaze darkened. "That's nice of you to say."

"It's the truth." He dug his hands into his pockets because all he wanted to do was grab her and kiss her and make her want more—as much as he did.

"I wish you'd stayed a little longer," he continued. "We could have had a good time in the morning, too."

"Mornings always complicate things, and we agreed to keep it simple."

"What if I wanted to change our agreement?"

She gave him a nervous look. "Change it to what?"

"I don't know, but one night wasn't enough. I'm certain of that."

"I'm still leaving, Devlin."

"Not for several more days. Why are we wasting the time that you're here?"

Before she could answer, heavy footsteps on the ramp drew his attention. His father was striding straight toward them. *Talk about lousy timing.*

Hannah stiffened when she saw Graham, but she didn't run. If anything, she squared her shoulders as if she were preparing for battle.

This was not what he wanted. But there was nothing he could do to stop it.

"Devlin, sorry I'm late." His father turned to Hannah, his gaze narrowing. "Where do I know you from?"

"I'm Hannah Reid, Mr. Blackthorne. I'm Frank's daughter."

His father's lips tightened. "Oh, of course, Hannah. I didn't realize you were in town."

"I thought my father needed me."

Graham cleared his throat. "Yes, well…" He turned to Devlin. "Are you ready to go?"

"Just waiting for you," he said, noting that his dad was dressed in jeans and a polo shirt, sneakers on his feet. He couldn't remember him looking so casual in a very long time.

"We'll see you out on the water," he told Hannah.

"As we fly by you," she returned, angry determination in her gaze.

As his dad moved toward the boat, Hannah stepped in front of him.

"Mr. Blackthorne," she said. "My father deserves his job back. He has been an incredibly loyal and devoted employee, and this personal fight between the two of you is hurting his livelihood. He needs to work, and you need him to work. He's the heart and soul of the Boatworks."

Graham gave her a hard look. "I can appreciate a daughter standing up for her father."

"I don't need you to appreciate me. I need you to appreciate my dad."

"This is between your father and me. You and Devlin need to stay out of it." Graham didn't wait for an answer, pushing past Hannah, and then climbing aboard and disappearing into the interior of the boat.

Hannah turned to him. "I know you didn't want me to say anything, Devlin. I just couldn't pretend nothing was wrong. I hope I didn't make things worse."

"I don't think you could do that," he said lightly, even though it was possible she'd done exactly that. On the other hand, she might have lit an even bigger fire underneath his father to take Frank out of the race. He'd have to see how it played out.

"I better go," she said.

"We're not done talking about us."

"Yes, we are."

As she walked away in her tight white jeans and soft blue sweater, her blonde hair bouncing around her shoulders, all he could think about was how tired he was of her leaving. She always seemed to be walking away from him.

Was he prepared to do what it might take to get her to stay?

The test run was turbulent and did not go as well as Devlin had hoped. He'd gotten used to his father being great at everything he did, but his sailing skills were average at best. He was out of practice, and he hadn't ever sailed a boat with as much technology as the *Wind Warrior*. He fumbled with the sails. He misjudged the wind. He almost fell into the ocean at one point. With every mistake, his father got more and more annoyed.

Things got worse when the *Daisy Mae* came into view.

The old boat didn't move through the water like the *Wind Warrior*. But damn if Frank and Hannah didn't sail by them with quite a bit of ease. While she gave him a wave, Frank refused to look in their direction. And then they were gone.

He changed direction as well, not wanting them to see that he and his father were not moving together as well as they should. They needed to work the kinks out on their own. But that wouldn't be easy. It wasn't just the sailing they had to conquer; it was all the unspoken tension between them.

He adjusted the sails and turned on the autopilot. It was past time to get rid of the tension. "Let's cruise for a while," he said.

His dad nodded. "I'd forgotten how challenging it is to race. I'm rusty."

"We have time for you to get better."

"I don't know if I have the time to put into this. I have a lot of balls in the air right now."

"There's no one else available."

"There has to be someone. Jason is back."

"And he told me quite pointedly that I'd be better off putting Nana on the boat."

His father gave him a faint smile. "That might be true."

"I think you should do it, Dad. I know today has been rough, but you're not a quitter."

His father stiffened, but then he nodded. "I suppose I deserve that. I said the same thing to you when you wanted to give up."

"What did I want to give up on?" he challenged. "I don't remember you ever saying that to me."

"I said it the night you told me you'd joined a yacht crew and were going to sail around the world. I thought you were quitting on the life you were supposed to have, the life you would have had if Amy hadn't died."

He was stunned to hear her name cross his father's lips. "I don't recall that conversation."

"You didn't want to hear anything back then. You were hurting too much. And it killed me and your mother that we couldn't help you."

"No one could help me."

"You had to deal with your grief in your own way," his father agreed. "But it wasn't easy to watch."

He didn't know what to say. He hadn't had this personal of a conversation with his father in years, maybe since before Amy had died. They'd talked mostly business the past few years or occasionally sports, but it hadn't gotten deeper than that.

"Getting back to today…" he said. "I'd like you to race with me. You must be a little tempted. You and Uncle Mark were unbeatable for years in this race. And this boat is top of the line. We can win."

Graham gave him a doubtful look. "I'm not so sure of that, and I don't want to lose to Frank. That would make him way too happy. If you want to show off the *Wind Warrior* and cross the finish line in first, then you need a skilled racer by your side."

It wasn't that his father was wrong, but there weren't many options. All the skilled racers were on other boats. "Well, you have one other choice, Dad. We can rehire Frank and put him back on this boat." He paused. "I meant what I told you a week ago, Dad. I won't run the company with my hands tied behind my back. If I'm in charge, I'm in charge. You've been stalling me for days, but this situation needs to be resolved one way or the other."

"You'd really walk away from the Boatworks, from the business you've built—for Frank?"

"Yes." He met his father's aggressive gaze. "Some things

—some people—are worth fighting for. Frank is one of them. You know that. It's his designs that bring our biggest customers to us. His craftsmanship and eye to detail is beyond compare. He has been incredibly loyal to the company, and we're going to lose him if we don't get him back now. He already interviewed with Victory Sailing."

"That company is nothing compared to ours."

"That's not the point. I know you're upset that Mom confided in Frank, but I have to know if there's more than that going on. If not, I think we can get past that."

"Frank had the nerve to tell me how to handle my marriage. It's not like he managed his own with any great expertise. I've been married for thirty-seven years. He made it less than twenty."

"I don't think it's a competition. Maybe he didn't want you to make the same mistakes he made. Hannah told me that her father chose work over her mother."

"I have never done that."

"Come on, Dad. You were doing a deal at her birthday party."

"I had other things planned; she left before they happened. And I honestly did not think it would bother her. It never has before."

"Or maybe it has, and you just haven't noticed."

"I told you that you and I are not discussing my relationship with your mother. You're not married or even in a relationship, so I'm not interested in your opinion."

"Fine. Then let's get back to Frank. I need an answer now." He thought he saw a glimmer of grudging respect in his father's eyes.

"All right. You can hire him back. He can race with you, and we'll go back to the way things were."

"Not exactly the way things were," he corrected. "The day-to-day operation of the Boatworks is my responsibility.

You need to stay out of it, especially when it comes to personnel matters. Can you do that?"

"I can do that, as long as you keep the company operating in the black."

"Then we have an agreement."

His father nodded. "Yes. And you better win that damn race after all this."

"I'm going to do my best." As the words came out of his mouth, he felt a twinge of guilt. If Frank agreed to come back on the *Wind Warrior*, then Hannah's dreams of racing with her dad would be shattered.

But wouldn't she be happy that her dad had his job back?

It was a trade-off, but he hoped she'd be willing to make that trade.

"What do you think, Dad?" Hannah asked as they put the *Daisy Mae* back into her slip.

"It went better than I thought. I need to make some adjustments in the sails. And we could work better together."

"We'll keep practicing. I know I'm not as skilled as Devlin, but I learn fast."

He gave her a small smile. "I know you do. And I have a feeling Devlin will have his hands full with Graham."

She nodded, having given him that piece of information before they'd gone out on the ocean.

They'd only seen the *Wind Warrior* for a minute. Apparently, Devlin had not wanted to sail anywhere within sight of them, which had been fine with her. She hadn't wanted him or his father to see them stumble in their training run. They already had enough of an advantage.

But she and her dad were used to being underdogs. They were up to the challenge.

At least, she hoped they were.

Because it had been really fun to sail with her dad again.

"We'll need to go out every day until the race," her father said. "We have to get more in sync as a team."

"We will. We have a shot at winning. It might be a long shot, but it's a shot."

"You were always competitive, even as a child."

"I take after you."

"And your mother. We all like to win."

"Guilty. I do have to say, though, that the *Wind Warrior* is an awesome boat. You did a great job on her, Dad."

"One of the best boats I've ever designed and built."

She inwardly winced at the hint of pain in his voice, and she wondered if Devlin had finally had a chance to have his conversation with his father. He was determined to get a final answer. She just hoped they were all ready for that answer, because based on what his father had said to her, she thought there was no chance of Graham Blackthorne backing down.

As they got off the boat, she saw Devlin walking in their direction. His expression seemed unusually serious, and his father was nowhere in sight, neither of which seemed to be a good thing.

"Frank, Hannah," he said. "How was your sail?"

"Great," she answered. "The *Daisy Mae* is a good boat."

"I'm sure she's better now that Frank has worked on her." He turned to her father. "I have good news, Frank. I want to hire you back. I realize that you may need added incentives after what happened, and we can talk about all that. But your job is yours. I hope you still want it."

She was surprised, but perhaps Graham had realized that Devlin was serious about leaving if her dad didn't come back.

"I'll have to think about it," her father said slowly.

"You need to think about it, Dad? Why?"

"Because I do," he said shortly.

"I want to assure you, Frank, that my dad will never ever have anything to do with personnel decisions again. He's agreed to give me complete autonomy over the Boatworks. I'm sorry it took this long to resolve matters, but it's been a crazy few weeks. I hope you know how much I want you back. And..." He shot her a quick look, then continued. "I'd like to have you race the *Wind Warrior* with me."

Her stomach turned over and now she understood the odd expression in his eyes. He felt guilty about killing her dreams. But that guilt hadn't stopped him from doing it. "My dad and I are racing together," she reminded him.

"Well, it's up to Frank, of course. But since he built the *Wind Warrior*, I wanted to give him the chance to race it."

"Your father knows he can't beat me," her dad said, a knowing gleam in his eyes. "He's out of practice. He doesn't want to lose. That's why he suddenly changed his mind about me."

"Is that true?" she asked.

"That my dad's skills are a little rusty, yes," Devlin replied. "But that didn't have anything to do with his decision regarding your job."

"Oh, I think it did," Frank said. "As I said, I need to consider my options."

Devlin didn't look happy with her father's answer. "All right. I just want to reiterate that the race is separate from the job. You can come back to work and still race with Hannah."

"Understood."

"Dad—" she started, thinking she needed to let him off the hook for the race. The *Wind Warrior* was his baby as much as it was Devlin's.

Her father put up a hand. "Please, no more words. I have some thinking to do, and you two need to let me do it. Can you get yourself home, Hannah?"

"Sure. But where are you going?"

"I'd like to be on my own for a while. We'll talk later."

As her father left, Devlin said, "I'm sorry, Hannah. I felt I had to offer Frank the opportunity to race the *Wind Warrior*."

"I know."

"And I hoped you'd be happy that I'm rehiring him."

"I'm thrilled he can have his job back, but I'm a little sad for myself. I know my father will feel compelled to race with you. Actually, compelled isn't even the right word, because he'll *want* to race with you. You are a much better sailor than I am. And the *Daisy Mae* doesn't hold a candle to the *Wind Warrior*."

"I told him the race is a separate deal."

"We'll see. The thing is, even if he agrees to sail with me, I should let him go. The two of you will be unbeatable, and the *Wind Warrior* will get all the glory. As you said, my dad built that boat. It's the way it should be." She paused. "Why did your father change his mind? When I spoke to him, I got the feeling he would never back down. Was it your ultimatum?"

"Maybe. I'd like to think he respects the job I'm doing."

"I'm sure he does."

"I have to say that, for the first time, I feel like the Boat-works might really be mine."

She could see the pleasure in his eyes and knew that meant a lot to him. "It's a win for you and for my dad."

"I don't want those wins to be at your expense," he said quietly. "I don't want to hurt you, Hannah."

"You're not hurting me. It's all good. This is the way it should be. This racing world belongs to you and my dad. I shouldn't have let myself get so caught up in it. What's important is that my father gets his life back and that his work is valued, not only by you and your family, but also by the sailing public. I know that the upcoming race is as much about business as it is about sailing."

"You're being very understanding."

"I'm trying to be."

"Do you think there's a chance your father will not come back to the Boatworks?"

"I honestly don't know, Devlin. I would have thought he'd say yes immediately."

"Do you know anything about an offer from Victory Sailing?"

"I know they made him one, but he hasn't shared the details. My father is a proud man, Devlin. I hope he doesn't let pride get in the way of making the best decision."

"Pride has been the problem throughout this whole situation—first from my father, now from yours. Good thing we are nothing like either one of them."

His small smile warmed her heart, and she felt a wave of yearning desire sweep through her. Memories of their night together ran through her head. There hadn't just been incredible pleasure but also laughter and honesty. With Devlin, she felt like she could be herself, and she hadn't felt that way in a long time.

"Let's get a drink or dinner," Devlin said.

His offer was incredibly tempting, but she was already having a difficult time letting go of Devlin. Spending more time with him wouldn't make it easier. "I can't."

Disappointment filled his gaze. "You're angry with me for breaking up the father-daughter duo."

"That's not it. I have to go."

He caught her by the arm, gazing into her eyes. "I don't want you to leave, Hannah."

"I don't see how I can stay," she whispered. "This isn't my home."

"You're happy here."

"I'm happy in Austin, too," she argued, trying not to let herself get caught up in the emotion of the moment, because she'd missed Devlin so much the past two days.

"Come home with me tonight. Let's talk this out. Let's be together."

"We said it would just be one night, and it was a great night. We both have a beautiful memory. Let's leave it at that," she said, barely getting the words out as emotion choked her throat. She pushed past him, praying he wouldn't come after her, because she didn't know if she could get herself to walk away again.

She held her breath all the way up the ramp, but when she finally turned her head, she realized he was gone. He'd let her go.

She should be happy about that.

CHAPTER FIFTEEN

WANTING to not only give her dad time to think about his options, but also to give herself a chance to burn off the painful emotions of the last few minutes, Hannah walked through the downtown area, stopping for a coffee before eventually heading home. She knew she'd made the right decision turning down Devlin's invitation, but being right didn't feel all that great. Still, she'd managed to pull herself together, and she had her game face on.

Her dad needed to say yes to taking his job back and yes to racing with Devlin. Both choices would bring him happiness, and that's what she wanted for him. Even if they didn't race together, they'd had fun today, and since she'd come back to King Harbor they had connected on a much deeper level. Their relationship was as strong as it had ever been, and she was grateful for that.

When she entered the house, her father was sitting at the dining room table, his laptop computer open in front of him, his reading glasses sliding halfway down his nose. At the closing of the door, he looked up and removed his glasses, his expression unreadable.

"I'm back," she said with a smile. "I hope it's not too soon. But I can go to my room if you want more alone time."

"No, it's fine. I'm sorry I made you walk home."

"I love to walk; you know that. No apology needed. It felt good." She pulled out a chair and sat down across from him. "Dare I ask if you've thought about Devlin's offer?"

"I've done nothing but think. I don't know, Hannah; I just don't know."

"What don't you know?" she asked curiously, surprised again by his hesitation.

"Whether I can trust Devlin when he says this will never happen again. Whether I should go back to a company that let me go. Whether I want to let Graham off the hook for what he did. And whether it might be time to make a break, do something new, start over."

She noticed he hadn't mentioned the race at all, but that was understandable. It was the last thing on his mind.

"That's a lot to consider," she murmured. "I think you can trust Devlin. This only took as long as it did because Claire walked out and shook everything up. Devlin didn't want to press his father when he was in a fragile place. But he did ultimately do it, and he put his own job on the line for you. He values you a great deal, and Devlin is the company, not Graham."

"That's true."

"As for the starting over part…do you still feel like you have enough challenge at the Boatworks? Do you need more money? I'm sure you could negotiate a raise and pretty much anything else you want now."

"I would definitely negotiate a salary increase. There are plenty of challenges in my job. Devlin gives me a great deal of autonomy."

"Because he respects you, Dad. There's no doubt about that."

Her father met her gaze. "What about the race?"

She drew in a breath at their moment of truth. "I think you should do it with Devlin. The *Wind Warrior* is your boat. And you two racing it together would be unbeatable."

"But you wanted to race with me."

"I did, but it's not like we can't sail again sometime. This is your life, Dad. It's the life you've built. The Boatworks, the race—they're part of it. I don't want to hold you back in any way. I want you to be happy."

"I want you to be happy, too. Okay. I know what I want to do." He picked up his phone.

"Do you want some privacy?"

"Not necessary. I'm going to tell Devlin that I'll take my job back with a significant pay increase and an extra two weeks of vacation time, so I can get out to Austin more often."

She was amazed by that statement. Her dad had only visited her a handful of times since she'd left. "That would be wonderful."

"I haven't always been the greatest father, Hannah. I'd like to say I did my best, but I don't think that's true, and I'm sure you don't think it's true, either."

"I wish we'd spent more time together after the divorce, but I know that our distance over the last five years has been as much my fault as yours. We can do better."

"Starting this weekend. I want to race with you, Hannah. Let's take on Devlin and Graham."

"Seriously? We're probably going to lose to them, maybe to a bunch of other boats as well."

"I have confidence we can hold our own."

She smiled at the sparkle in his eyes. "I'm game, but I don't want you to feel like you'd be letting me down if you chose to race with Devlin. I completely understand the situation, and I'm good with it."

"Well, I'm not. The only thing I'm good with is you and me racing to the finish line together, with Devlin and

Graham in our wake. But we'll need to practice every day until then."

"I'm ready. I wish we could go now."

He laughed. "Tomorrow will do."

"I'll make dinner, while you talk to Devlin," she said, getting to her feet. She felt ridiculously happy that her father had finally chosen her over everything else. She was also glad she wouldn't have to leave King Harbor just yet.

Devlin walked into his father's study Tuesday night. His dad was studying some reports, a whisky by his hand.

"I have some news." He took a seat in the chair in front of his father's massive mahogany desk.

"Good news, I hope."

"Frank has agreed to come back to the Boatworks at a 20 percent increase in salary."

Graham rolled his eyes. "Frank always acts like he's so much better than me, but he's not. He saw an advantage, and he went for it."

"As you would," he pointed out. "Since I think he deserves compensation for the past two weeks of stress, I agreed."

"It's your company."

"Yes, it is. Frank also told me that he's not going to race with me."

Surprise flashed across his father's face. "Are you serious? Why the hell not? He built that boat. He has told me a number of times that it's his baby."

"His real baby is Hannah, and he's going to race with her on the *Daisy Mae*. He said he'd made her a promise, and he was not going to let her down again." He actually felt good about Frank's decision. Hannah deserved her day on the ocean with her father. Plus, that meant she couldn't leave

King Harbor until at least Monday, which was also excellent news.

"Well, Frank can't beat you with that boat or his daughter."

"He's worked on the boat and Hannah is a great sailor."

"How would you know that?" his father asked, a curious gleam in his eyes.

"I took her out one day."

"Interesting."

"What's more interesting is that I still don't have someone to race with unless you change your mind."

"Come on, Devlin. There are plenty of guys at the Boatworks who will race with you."

"Not really, and I want to race with you."

"Why? You saw how rusty I was."

"We'll go out tomorrow, Thursday, and Friday. You'll be ready by Saturday."

"I have other things to attend to."

"You can fit this in—if you want to."

His dad settled back in his chair. "I don't know why you're pushing so hard. I might be a liability."

"I'd rather lose with you than win with someone else."

"Seriously?"

"You're my father. I've wanted to race with you for years. I know it's painful for you, that the race brings back memories of Uncle Mark. But it's time to make new memories. Beating Frank could be one of them."

"You know the right button to push."

"Is that a yes?"

"Yes."

"Good. I'll meet you at the dock at two." He got up, then paused. "And so we're clear, Dad—I'm in charge on the boat. You follow my directions. I'm team leader."

His dad laughed. "Don't push it Devlin."

He smiled back at him, feeling a connection to his father

for the first time in a long time. Hopefully the race would enhance that, but that might depend on whether they won or not.

The ocean was crowded with racers all week, but Devlin still caught glimpses of Hannah and Frank out on the *Daisy Mae*. They were getting better; he could see it in their runs. But he and his father were also improving. His dad had gotten back into the groove of racing, and while they'd hit a few control issues, for the most part, his father had followed his direction.

As he motored through the harbor after completing their final practice run late Friday afternoon, he had to admit it felt good to be better at something than his dad, who had always been so successful at everything he did. But on the boat, they were equals.

They hadn't talked much while sailing, concentrating on the techniques that would make them faster. The topic of his mother had remained off-limits. He knew his dad had someone keeping tabs on her, but other than that, he'd made no attempt to try to resolve the separation.

His hope that his mother would come back for the race was quickly diminishing. In years past, she'd hosted the pre-race Friday night cocktail party at the Yacht Club, but tonight his dad would do that alone.

After docking the boat, they disembarked just in time to run into Frank and Hannah.

"How was your sail?" he asked.

"Perfect," Frank replied shortly, his gaze moving to Graham. "You got your sea legs yet, Graham?"

"Never lost them," Graham retorted. "I hear you've negotiated a nice raise for yourself."

"Only what I'm due. You would have done the same. Hell, you would have asked for three times more than I did."

"Very true. I always shot higher than you. That's how I got Claire."

"You got her, but can you keep her? That's the question."

Devlin inwardly groaned at Frank's words, and he could see worry flash through Hannah's eyes as well, but their fathers were not paying them any attention.

"I'll keep her, because she's mine," Graham said, a fierce tone in his voice. "I'm her husband. She loves me."

"She does love you," Frank agreed. "And she needs you. That's all I was trying to tell you, Graham, but you couldn't hear me. You were blinded by unnecessary anger and way too much ego. I'm not your enemy; you are. You need to get out of your own way. And I say that because I know what it feels like to lose the woman you love because you can't do that. Now, if you want to fire me again for trying to help you, go ahead."

Graham gave Frank a hard stare and then turned away, moving up the ramp at a brisk pace, his back poker-stiff, his head held high in the air.

"Sorry, Devlin, I had to speak the truth," Frank said. "If you want to break our new agreement—"

"I don't," he interrupted. "I told you before, I'm in charge of the Boatworks. The problems you and my father have are your own."

"Fair enough. I'll see you both at the party."

"And then there were two," Hannah said, as Frank walked away.

He gazed into her eyes, fighting off a powerful aching urge to pull her into his arms and never let her go. But she wasn't his to keep.

And what the hell was he going to do come Monday when she was gone for good?

"You look beautiful," he murmured. "A little sunburned."

She put a hand to her pink cheeks. "I do feel warm." Her

lips curved into a wistful smile. "But that tends to happen when you're around."

"I know the feeling." He paused. "You also look happy. I'm glad your father decided to race with you."

"Me, too. Whatever happens tomorrow, it's all good. Not that I don't want to win. But I know the odds are against us."

"The race is always unpredictable. You can plan and practice, try to anticipate every scenario, but when you're racing, it's all about split-second decisions, feeling the rhythm of the boat, the turn of the wind, the movements of your racing partner. You have to be willing to leave it all on the ocean, risk everything for the win. And I know you're capable of doing that. So is Frank."

"How do you know that about me? It's not like I've lived an adventurous, pushing-the-envelope kind of life. I haven't sailed around the world like you."

"No. But you put your life on hold to rush to your father's side. You had the courage to challenge my father, and not many people stand up to Graham Blackthorne."

"I did do that, but I think it was you standing up that made the difference."

"I saw my actions through your eyes, and I didn't like them, Hannah."

She gave him a thoughtful look. "You never said that before."

"I should have rehired Frank the second after my father fired him. I'm sorry I didn't."

"You were in a difficult position. Family is complicated. How are you and your dad getting along in terms of racing?"

"Not bad, actually. His skills are coming back, and we haven't been arguing at all. What about you?"

"We're getting along better than ever. We had a breakthrough in our relationship the past few weeks. I think my dad losing his job actually made him rethink his entire life, all the decisions he made in the past, what he wants for the future. Sometimes we all need a big shove out the door to actually go into the world and see what we might be missing."

"That's true." He might need that shove, too. He'd gotten into a well-worn and way-too-comfortable rut, but Hannah coming back to King Harbor had turned his life upside down, made him think that maybe he wanted more than what he had.

But how much more? And did he have the courage to put his heart on the line again?

"I guess I should go," she said, a reluctant note in her voice. "The cocktail party will be starting soon. I assume you're going."

"I always have," he muttered, but going to that party was actually the last thing he wanted to do.

"I'm sure it's expected since the Blackthornes are one of the race sponsors."

"My father can represent the family. So can yours. Why don't we play hooky?"

"What do you have in mind?"

"Dinner at my apartment. I can grill a mean steak."

Mixed emotions played through her eyes. "I should say no. We're rivals. We're going to be battling each other tomorrow…"

"But?"

"I've missed you."

Her soft admission made his body tighten. "Then come home with me. Tomorrow, we can be competitors. Tonight, we can just be together."

"That sounds…"

"Perfect?"

Her smile lit up her pretty blue eyes. "Yeah, perfect. I guess our fling could go another night."

"Absolutely," he said, but he was starting to think he wanted much more than a fling.

CHAPTER SIXTEEN

IT WAS both the longest and the shortest ride to Devlin's apartment. Hannah felt more than a little conflicted. She wanted to be with Devlin, but she was very afraid that one more night was only going to make it more difficult to leave. But she'd been fighting her feelings for the better part of a week and she just didn't want to fight anymore.

Tomorrow was the race. By Monday she'd be gone. But she had tonight, and she wanted to make the most of it.

When they entered the apartment, the simmering tension between them exploded. And there was no more thought of dinner, only of each other. Their clothes came off fast and furiously, leaving a trail from the front door to the bedroom.

And when her head hit the bed, his hand was right there to cushion the fall. His mouth covered hers with passion and desperation, igniting her own raging emotions. Their time was limited. She wanted to make the most of every second.

Making love felt more intense now, more important than before. There seemed to be meaning behind every kiss, every touch, every heated look between them.

They moved fast and then slow, but they were always in sync, soaring higher and higher, in the end creating a blazing fire of passion that left her immensely satisfied and both physically and emotionally spent.

Devlin rolled on to his back with a happy sigh. She turned onto her side, gazing at his handsome face, the lips that had just tasted and teased every part of her body, making her feel wanted and needed in a way she'd never felt before.

He looked at her and smiled. "That was something."

"Something crazy," she agreed, running her fingers down his sculpted chest, feeling the heat and the sweat clinging to his skin.

He cupped his hand around her neck and pulled her down for a long, savoring kiss.

And when she lifted her head, she felt breathless again. "I hope you don't need a long break."

"All I need is you. Will you stay the night, Hannah?"

"Do I need to say yes in order to get my steak?"

He laughed. "Yes, that is a requirement."

"And you're really good at barbecuing?"

"The best. I can grill some vegetables, too, open up a bottle of wine… We can eat under the stars."

She didn't think she'd ever gotten such a good invitation. "I like the sound of all of that. But not just yet."

"You have something else in mind?"

She nodded. "I do."

His gaze darkened. "Want to tell me?"

She couldn't find the words to tell him what she was thinking. Or maybe she could find them, but she was too afraid of saying them aloud. She'd played it safe so much of her life. She'd always tried to be the good girl, hoping that in some way that would put her family back together, or at the very least it would make her mother lose her sad smile and encourage her father to want to see her.

But this wasn't about them; this was about her, what she wanted in her life—*who* she wanted in her life. Loving Devlin could be a huge risk. He had an ex haunting his life, too. He might suddenly remember how great Amy was and how she paled in comparison.

"Hannah? You can talk to me," Devlin said, his eyes filling with concern.

"I wish that neither of us had a history, that we were a clean slate before now, but we're not."

"I'm not him—the guy who said he wanted you but then changed his mind."

"I know." She could have added that he wasn't even close to being Gary, because at least Gary had wanted to make a commitment to her, even if he quickly realized it wasn't right. Devlin had never said anything beyond "Come home with me tonight. Be with me now".

"But something is bothering you," he said, his gaze troubled, as he pushed a strand of hair off her face.

"No. Everything is good." She wasn't going to mess up the last night they'd have together with worries about a future that she already knew wouldn't happen.

"I don't think I believe you, Hannah. You have very expressive eyes."

"Which should be showing you how happy I am."

"But also concerned. You're not really a fling kind of woman, are you?"

"No, but I'm glad I chose to fling myself at you." Her smile coaxed his grin back onto his lips.

"One good fling deserves another," he said, moving so suddenly she found herself on her back with Devlin's body coming down on hers, and every little doubt and worry fled her mind. She'd think later. Now, she was just going to feel.

She was gone—again. Devlin woke up to the alarm he'd remembered to set sometime in the middle of the night. But

Hannah was no longer curled up next to him in bed, and judging by the silence in his apartment, she'd left.

Just once he wanted to say good-bye to her.

Actually, that wasn't true. Good-bye was the last thing he wanted to say to her.

But they could have said other things. He could have made her breakfast since dinner had turned into heated-up pizza bites and a bowl of fruit sometime after midnight when they'd finally made it out of bed and into the kitchen. He'd promised her barbecue another night. *But would they get another night?* It didn't seem likely. Not unless one of them decided to make a big change.

He couldn't move to Austin; his entire life was here.

She probably felt that she couldn't move to King Harbor because her life was in Austin.

Was it really just about geography?

Or was it about being willing to make a commitment, to putting it all on the line? He'd always given everything when it came to work, to racing, but relationships… He'd told himself that was different. *But was it?*

With too many questions going around in his head, he got out of bed and headed for the shower. He couldn't think about Hannah now. He had a race to win, and very soon she would be one of his competitors, someone he needed to beat.

That wouldn't be easy. Winning would be good for his business and for his relationship with his dad, but winning would also be great for Frank, who had taken a beating the last few weeks, and for Hannah, who wanted to show her dad that he could win with her.

But one of them was not going to win. And there was a part of him that wished the race was over already. *But then what?*

He had a feeling that even if he won the race, he was going to end up a loser.

Stepping out of the shower, he threw on his clothes and

headed into the kitchen to grab a banana and a protein bar. When he saw the note taped to his refrigerator, he couldn't help but smile.

Good luck Devlin. May the best woman win.

He touched his fingers to the smiley face she'd drawn next to her name. He hoped he'd have another chance to make her smile one more time. But it probably wouldn't be at the end of the race, not if he came in first.

"Nervous?" her father asked, as they motored out of the harbor to the starting line.

"A little," she admitted.

"That's good. Nerves are part of this experience. You're about to test yourself. It's exciting."

"And a little terrifying. I don't want to let you down."

"You couldn't. It's just a race, Hannah; it's not the beginning or the end of anything."

"You're right," she said. But she didn't really agree, because it did feel like something was ending. Only that feeling had nothing to do with the race.

In the distance, she could see Devlin and Graham on the *Wind Warrior*. Devlin looked so damn good on his boat. He was truly at home on the sea. He could never live away from the ocean. King Harbor was where he belonged. And she was starting to wonder if she belonged here, too.

But if she made the choice to move, that didn't necessarily mean that she and Devlin would be together. He'd locked his heart away a long time ago.

Would he unlock it for her? And would she be too afraid to find out?

The safest thing for her to do was to go home and live her life.

But did she want to be safe?

"If you want him, Hannah, you should make it happen," her dad said, tipping his head toward Devlin's boat.

"It takes two for that."

"I don't think the feelings are one-sided."

"But you warned me before that Devlin goes through women like water."

"He used to. He's been different these past two weeks. I think he finally met a woman he wants to keep."

Her heart soared at that possibility. "What if he doesn't?"

"Only one way to find out. But you're going to have to do that later. Right now, you need to focus on beating him."

"I will. I still want this win for us."

"Then let's go get it."

CHAPTER SEVENTEEN

THE OCEAN WAS CROWDED with sailboats, the sea choppy, the wind currently at about 12 knots but predicted to rise to 20 knots, making for an exciting, fast race. Crowds of people were on the bluffs, where they'd get a good view of the action. But there was no better place than where he was. Devlin's heart beat faster as they prepared for the start. Adrenaline was flowing through his body, but he needed to keep that under control. Excitement was good, but calm was necessary to win.

As he shifted his feet, his gaze moved to the *Daisy Mae*, and seeing Hannah sent a different wave of excitement through him. He needed to get a handle on that, too. In fact, he needed to look away, because she was a distraction he could not afford.

"Are you sure you have it in you to win this race?" Graham asked.

"What?" He looked at his father in confusion and annoyance. "Why would you ask me that?"

"Because you haven't taken your eyes off the *Daisy Mae*, and I don't think it's the boat drawing your attention. I doubt it's Frank, either. But that pretty blonde…" He paused. "You like her. I thought I saw something in your eyes yesterday, but now I know I did."

"Hannah is amazing," he muttered. "But I'm not going to hand this race to her."

"And you don't feel like you owe Frank for the hell I put him through?"

"I'm glad you finally see that you were in the wrong."

"I didn't say that."

"Well, I have no intention of losing this race. I want us to win. And if Hannah and Frank want the trophy, they're going to have to beat us."

"Good, because I don't play to lose."

"Neither do I."

"Maybe you're more like me than you think, Devlin."

"I don't know that anyone is like you, Dad," he said dryly.

"Good point. I've never wanted to be like anyone else, and neither have you. You've always been comfortable in your own skin, pursuing your own dreams. I respect that."

"Thank you." He was surprised by the compliment, but he'd take it.

"How long is Hannah staying in town?"

"Only another day or two."

"And you're just going to let her go?"

"You're one to talk about not letting women go," he couldn't help pointing out.

His father frowned. "My situation is completely different. Claire and I have been together for thirty-seven years. We will get past this."

"I hope so. Anyway, it's showtime. Are you ready to do this?"

"I'm ready."

His heart began to race…and they were off…

For the first sixty minutes, the boats were bunched together, but eventually they began to separate, the novices falling behind, the pros soaring ahead. The *Daisy Mae* was keeping up with the *Wind Warrior*, but there were three other boats on their tail as well. But he didn't have time to think about his competition. Right now, it was about the boat and the sea, flying through the waves with precision and fearlessness.

Two hours into the race, his muscles were straining. The wind was fierce now, the waves bigger than any he'd ever raced.

His dad had been moving with agile efficiency, but he seemed to be slowing down.

"We're almost there," he yelled in encouragement. "We've got this."

In the last five minutes, the field had narrowed to two—the *Wind Warrior* and the *Daisy Mae*. He'd always known it would come down to the two of them.

It was close, but they were edging ahead. They could do it. They could win.

And then his father stumbled. The sail shifted. It took less than a minute to recover, but it was sixty seconds too long.

He was stunned to see the *Daisy Mae* shoot across the finish line by half a boat length.

It was over.

They'd lost.

But when he looked over and saw Hannah and Frank hugging, he couldn't help but appreciate their joy. They'd both needed the win, and they'd gotten it.

"Sorry, Devlin," his dad said, putting his hand on his shoulder. "I don't know what happened. I guess I lost my concentration for a second. This is on me."

Had his father just slipped? There was something in his father's tone that made him wonder. *On the other hand, why would he have thrown the race?* He'd wanted to beat Frank even more than he did.

Clearing his throat, he said, "No. This is not on you. Win or lose, we did it together. And I'm happy we did."

His father met his gaze. "You're a hell of a sailor, Devlin, but you're an even better son. Your Uncle Mark would have loved seeing you race like this. In truth, he was always better than me. He was the reason we won all those trophies."

"You never said that before."

"I'm not the most humble man, in case you hadn't noticed."

He laughed. "I've noticed."

His dad surprised him once more with a hug. And then they took the *Wind Warrior* home.

Her arms were aching, her legs shaking from the stress of the last few hours, but Hannah felt incredibly happy. She'd never really thought they could win, but they had.

"I still can't believe we did it," Hannah said, as they brought the *Daisy Mae* into port.

"The old girl raced better than I thought she would," her father admitted. "And you weren't bad, either."

"Thank you. But it was all you. You were amazing."

"I didn't think we had it. Devlin was right there. The win was his. Something happened."

"What happened is that we crossed the finish line in front of them."

"That's right," he said, but there was something in his gaze that made her frown.

"But that's not what you really think?"

"Honestly, I don't know, Hannah. But I've sailed for years with Devlin, and if he has a lead that close to the finish, he doesn't let it go."

"Maybe he got tired, or his dad did, but whatever—we won. And I want to celebrate."

"We will definitely do that. I'm going to lift that trophy high and hopefully right in Graham's face."

She smiled, but the last thing she wanted to do was rub their win in Devlin's face. She knew the loss would sting, probably more because he would have lost with his dad. And that would hurt.

As they got off the boat, the other racers were waiting to congratulate them. Words of praise washed over her in a warm, rosy haze. She felt like she was floating. And her dad seemed taller than he had before, as if he could hold his head up again. He'd needed this win, and she'd helped him get it.

They didn't see Devlin and Graham until they lined up for the awards ceremony, and then they were on opposite sides of the big trophy. Devlin smiled and mouthed, *Congratulations*.

She was relieved that he didn't look too upset, but she wouldn't have expected him to be anything less than a gracious loser.

After speeches and the trophy presentation, the four of them posed for photos. It was crazy to think that two weeks ago, Frank and Graham had not even been on speaking terms, but now there was a thaw in the ice between them. They weren't being super friendly, but the level of animosity had dimmed.

When everything was over, they were congratulated by Fiona Blackthorne as well as Devlin's cousin, Jason, both of whom were extremely complimentary and had perhaps even enjoyed the fact that Graham had to deal with a loss. It was extremely rare for Graham Blackthorne to lose, and she was secretly thrilled to have been the one to help make that happen.

As Fiona and Jason moved on, the four of them had their first real chance to speak to each other.

"Well, Frank, looks like you finally beat me," Graham said.

Her father looked Graham straight in the eye. "You ran a good race, better than I expected."

"I'm sure you didn't expect much." Graham paused, then extended his hand. "Congratulations."

Her father hesitated, then shook Graham's hand. "Thank you. And from here on out, just so you know, I'll keep my mouth shut when it comes to you and Claire. You were right; it was none of my business."

Graham nodded. "You were right, too. I just didn't want to hear you. Why don't I buy you a drink?"

Hannah watched in shock as the two men made their way to the bar. "Well, that just happened. Are they friends again?"

Devlin laughed. "Looks that way."

She shook her head in bemusement. "That's crazy."

"Can we take a walk, Hannah? Get out of here? Or maybe you want to stay and celebrate? In fact, that's exactly what you should do." He shook his head, as if annoyed at himself. "Sorry, I don't know what I was thinking. This is your moment. Soak it up."

"It's more my dad's moment," she said, watching her father and Graham shaking hands with more competitors. "I'm so happy for him."

"You did it, too, Hannah."

"I know, and I'm proud of myself. But it was never about the trophy. Let's take a walk."

A happy gleam entered his eyes as they moved toward the door.

It took them about fifteen minutes to actually get out of the club, but eventually they made their way down the sidewalk and walked toward a path that wound its way around the bluffs. The hills were empty now that the race was over, but she could still hear the distant cheers as they'd sailed into first.

Despite Devlin saying he wanted to talk, he was remarkably quiet, although he did take her hand, squeezing her fingers as if that would somehow convey whatever he needed her to know. But she wasn't sure what he was trying to get across. Was he leading into a conversation that would involve words like *fun*, *we had a good time*, and *let's stay in touch*?

She wasn't sure she was ready for that. But whatever was coming, she needed to hear it. When they came upon a bench, she motioned for Devlin to sit down with her.

"This is good," she said. "My legs and arms are aching. I'm going to be sore tomorrow."

"But it will have been worth it."

"It was great to win. I felt empowered in a way I haven't felt in a long time. I think that's because I haven't put myself to that kind of physical and mental test in years. It was exciting and grueling."

"I'm glad you won."

"Well, I'm sorry you lost."

He smiled. "It's just a race. There will be another one next year."

"That's true. You and my dad can reunite."

"Or…you and I could do it together."

Her heart skipped a beat. "You want me to race with you a year from today?"

He slowly nodded. "I think we'd make a good team, too."

"But you don't look that far into the future."

"I do now." He paused, shifting sideways so that he was facing her. "I don't like waking up and having you be gone, Hannah."

"I thought it would be easier that way."

"You always think that, but it's not."

"I'm sorry. I did leave you a note."

He gave her a faint smile. "I appreciated that."

"I guess I wanted to avoid good-bye."

"I want to avoid it, too. Is there any chance you'd consider moving to King Harbor?"

Her breath caught in her chest at the question, at the intense, determined look in his eyes. "Are you sure you want that?"

"Yes. I'm falling in love with you, Hannah. Actually, I don't think I'm still falling; I've already hit the ground. You have knocked me off my feet. And I don't want to go a day without seeing you."

She could hardly believe what she was hearing. "But it was supposed to be a fling, a casual thing. You like things simple."

"I used to. I thought not caring too much would prevent me from having to walk through pain again. But I've been in pain the last week. The thought of not seeing you again, not being with you—it physically hurts. I know it's a lot to ask. You have your mother, your business, and your life in Austin. It would be difficult for me to move, but if that's what needs to happen, then I'll find a way to work it out."

"You have to be by the ocean. It's where your company is, and you make boats."

"Your father lost his wife to work. My father might have lost his for the same reason. I do not want to follow in either of their footsteps. I think we could have something great."

"I do, too," she whispered. "And you don't have to move to Austin, because I want to come home. King Harbor has always been the home of my heart. I can sell real estate anywhere. And there's this pretty house on the hill I have my eye on."

"It hasn't sold yet."

"How do you know that?" she asked in surprise.

"I called Kathy yesterday. I was curious. I was thinking I might buy it, use it as added leverage to get you to stay."

"You'd buy me a house to do that?"

"I'd buy you the whole damn world, Hannah." He framed her face with his hands. "I want you to be happy. I want us to have a committed, exclusive relationship. And I can promise you that nothing about that makes me want to panic. It actually brings me a feeling of incredible calm. You and I—we're right for each other. I know it."

"I know it, too. You make me happy, Devlin. And I would like to be in a committed, exclusive, and very hot relationship with you. See how I added the word *hot*?"

He laughed and kissed her. "Oh, baby, we are definitely hot. We are on fire."

She grinned back at him, feeling happier than she ever had before. "Let's go back to your place. You still owe me a steak."

"You don't want to celebrate with your dad?"

"I don't think he'll miss me. He told me before the race that if I wanted you in my life, I should make it happen. So, I'm going to make it happen. You are an incredible man, Devlin Blackthorne."

"That's not what you said the first time you saw me."

"Because I didn't know you." She gazed deep into his eyes. "But now I do. And if I'm going to risk my heart on anyone, I want it to be you."

He took her hand and put it on his chest. "My heart is yours."

"I'll take good care of it," she promised, as she pressed her lips against his.

THE END

Don't miss any of the Blackthornes!

7 BRIDES FOR 7 BLACKTHORNES

Devlin – Barbara Freethy (#1)
Jason – Julia London (#2)
Ross – Lynn Raye Harris (#3)
Phillip – Cristin Harber (#4)
Brock – Roxanne St. Claire (#5)
Logan – Samantha Chase (#6)
Trey – Christie Ridgway (#7)

Want more Barbara Freethy Books?

Check out my new series!

WHISPER LAKE

Always With Me (#1)
My Wildest Dream (#2)

For a complete list of books, visit www.barbarafreethy.com

ABOUT THE AUTHOR

 Barbara Freethy is a #1 New York Times Bestselling Author of 68 novels ranging from contemporary romance to romantic suspense and women's fiction. With over 12 million copies sold, twenty-three of Barbara's books have appeared on the New York Times and USA Today Bestseller Lists, including SUMMER SECRETS which hit #1 on the New York Times!

Known for her emotional and compelling stories of love, family, mystery and romance, Barbara enjoys writing about ordinary people caught up in extraordinary adventures.